Perfect Kiss

Mason Creek #9

USA Today Bestselling Author
Lacey Black

♡ Lacey
Black

Lacey Black

Perfect Kiss

Mason Creek #9

Editing by Kara Hildebrand

Proofreading by Joanne Thompson & Karen Hrdlicka

Format by Brenda Wright, Formatting Done Wright

Lacey Black

Chapter ONE

Malcolm

If there's one thing I dislike about city council meetings, it's sitting beside Betsy.

Betsy Reed filled her husband's unexpired term more than a decade ago, after Bernie passed away, and has been elected to the seat ever since. She's a sweet ol' lady with the best flower garden in town, but she's just a tad on the...smelly side. A combination of mothballs used where she stores her forty-year-old pantsuits and the cheapest perfume known to man, probably popular during the JFK dynasty, makes for a nauseating meeting.

Plus, she's a hugger. No amount of sexual harassment policies or mandatory training videos will stop her. Believe me, we've tried. But the woman is just overly friendly and has to hug. Everyone. All the time.

"Well, if you'll excuse me," I announce, pardoning myself from the small group of council members who stayed after the meeting to visit. Usually, I'd be right there with them, but not tonight. I'm in desperate need of some fresh air.

I head down the hall until I reach my office, the gold-plated sign reading Mayor Malcolm Wright displayed prominently on the door. That's me. Mayor of Mason Creek. I'm a third-generation mayor, both my father and grandfather holding the position before me. Unlike them, however, I'm not married with a child while holding the office. Much to their dismay, I'm married to my career with my sights set on something bigger and better.

Senator.

But let's not get ahead of myself. Right now, I'm content learning the ins and outs of local government and enjoying the single life and all it has to offer.

And damn, does it have a lot to offer.

If you know what I mean.

I step inside the small bathroom in my office and change my clothes. From a suit and tie to running shorts and a T-shirt. My Italian loafers are exchanged for Nike runners. I grab my phone and my earbuds and head for the back door.

Fortunately, there's no one in this part of the building. Everyone is congregating toward the front, where the city offices are located, including the large boardroom used by the council and committees. I'm able to stretch for my run in peace and quiet, even though my mind is stuck on an aged building code I've been trying to push for updating. If I'm going to get support to release the sidewalk restrictions in town, I'm going to have to get the business owners involved.

The city implemented an ordinance decades ago that businesses can't set up merchandise or displays on city-owned sidewalks. The thought was it causes fall risks for those utilizing the walkways. However, I see it differently. If a business were to tastefully display their products outside, it's a draw, not only for those walking by, but also on the streets. It's a form of advertising, much like their big window displays, and I know the local business owners would be thrilled with the idea.

I just have to rally some support.

Maybe I'll corner a few at the next Chamber of Commerce gathering in the park. That's prime opportunity to discuss my ideas with those who will benefit the most.

I set out at a grueling pace, quickly moving through the streets as the miles tick by. Of course, I make sure to avoid certain roads. There's a woman over on Oak Street who said she'd rather see a buffalo eating my rotting carcass than me in a grocery store aisle, and another over on Yount Avenue who hopes my balls get a horrible flesh-eating fungus and fall off.

Since I'm particularly fond of my balls, I avoid her like the plague.

I feel like I'm living in that George Strait song about his exes living in Texas. Except, all of mine live in Mason Creek, Montana.

That's what you get when you're a sworn bachelor in a small town of just under three thousand. I've always loved Mason Creek. It's actually full of rich history, something I've always found fascinating. It's a great place, where everyone knows you and waves as you pass.

It's also a place where, because everyone knows you, they know everything about you. The good, the bad, and the ugly. And when you're a sworn bachelor, burning through all the single ladies in the county, there tends to be your fair share of ugly.

Like Miss Flesh-Eating Fungus Lady. I heard about it at the post office. And the bank. And the grocery store. And that was before noon.

After pounding out a quick four miles, I wind my way back to the heart of town, where City Hall lies. I walk the remaining block to my destination, past my attorney's office, the bank, ice cream stand, and the fountain until I'm finally where I started. I do a few more stretches, noticing the streets are now empty, the stragglers from tonight's meeting gone home.

I let myself in and make my way to my office. I notice the light on in the conference room and make a mental note to shut it off before I leave. Right now, all I can think about is taking a shower. Between the residual mothball scent that seems to stick to my skin every month and the BO from my run, I'm desperate to wash up.

Fortunately, there's a small bathroom with a shower in my office. I have no idea why. No one seems to know. It was there when my grandfather took the office more than two decades ago, and no one seemed to remember why it was put in.

But I'm not going to argue. It's times like these I'm grateful as hell to have a shower. It comes in handy on late nights or early mornings, both of which I've had during my short time as Mayor of Mason Creek. I can move from the Wright and Son Law Office to here easily and vice versa and still get in my daily run.

I make it work.

Before my grandfather was the mayor, he started his own law firm. Family law, mostly. Divorces, child custody cases, restraining orders, and spousal maintenance and property. It wasn't until my dad joined him years later—hence the Wright and Son name—that more business and bankruptcy law services were offered, and now with me joining the business, we've incorporated my passion for wills, estate planning, and probate too.

I toe off my running shoes near my desk and pad toward the bathroom, dropping my sweaty shirt on the floor as I go. When I'm in the bathroom, I turn on the hot water and strip off the rest of my clothes. The water feels amazing, scalding, yet soothing my overworked and achy muscles.

I take a quick shower, scrubbing off the run, before stepping out onto the tile floor. There are a handful of towels on a shelf, so I grab one and start to dry my body. Just as I move the terrycloth to my back, the bathroom door flies open and in walks a woman.

A very beautiful woman.

Her wide hazel eyes meet mine before dropping. I can tell the moment they land on my groin, because they enlarge even farther, almost comically so. Like a cartoon. Except there's nothing funny about what's suddenly happening to my cock. It has definitely taken a strong interest in the double-X chromosome in the room.

When those hypnotic orbs find mine, she gasps, dropping whatever's in her hand. A spray bottle of some sort and maybe a cleaning rag, but I can't be sure. My own eyes are glued to hers, like watching the sun set over the ocean, I'm completely enthralled.

Even if I'm standing here buck ass naked.

"Holy shit, I'm so sorry," she bellows, bringing her hands up to her eyes to shield them.

A lot of good that'll do. She's already seen the goods.

"It's okay," I insist, taking a step forward and resting my towel on my shoulders.

"I didn't know anyone was still here," she insists quickly, still covering her eyes with her hand.

I take a moment to enjoy the view. She's average height with her hair pulled into a tight ponytail. It's brown and is begging for my fingers to tangle in those long locks. She's got the cutest button nose and her lips are plump and ripe for kissing.

But that's not what holds my attention now. It's that damn hourglass figure that should be illegal in this state. Large tits that beg to be freed from their confines and the most delicious ass I've ever seen. My cock definitely takes notice and appreciates the view very much.

If I'm not careful, I'm going to need another shower; this time a very cold one.

"Mr. Mayor. Sir. I'm so sorry for..." She waves her hand at the door and then at me, all while holding the other hand up to her face, and I have to fight to keep the grin at bay.

"Well, you seem to have me at a disadvantage. And you are?" I ask, amused to find her eyes peeking through the crack of her fingers.

"Lenora Abbott. Leni," she states, taking a step back, as if looking to make a hasty retreat. "Sir."

I can't help but smirk. I hate it when people call me sir, but hearing this woman say it, her voice full of nervousness and shock, well, I suddenly don't seem to mind at all.

Ahh, yes. Lenora Abbott. She was about six years younger than me in school, and even though we didn't hang in the same circles, it's a small enough town that I recognize the name right away. Plus, I've seen her out and about a few times since her return. No one slips into Mason Creek without everyone taking notice.

"Well, Lenora Abbott, I have to admit, you've caught me by surprise," I tease, leaving the towel across my shoulders and making absolutely no attempt to cover my groin. Why would I when she's eyeing it like a slice of birthday cake she can't wait to devour.

It's as if the lights truly click on in her gorgeous head, and unfortunately, she starts to retreat. Quickly. "I'm so sorry," she parrots, walking backward until she runs into the doorframe. "Ouch. I'll just...go. To the other bathroom. Start there. Clean. Without you being...naked."

I can't help but smile. She's fucking adorable as she stammers and sputters, trying to get away, yet snatching little glimpses of me before she goes. "Sounds good, Lenora. I'll only be a few more minutes, and then this bathroom is all yours."

She nods and is gone a moment later, leaving behind quite the first impression and me with a growing erection I'll have to deal with later. But right now isn't the time. Right now, I need to get dressed, and even though I should be heading home for the night, I might just hang around. Find something to do in my office. Steal a few more moments with one Lenora Abbott.

I already know it's a bad idea, but I can't help myself.

I want more.

Chapter TWO

Leni

I practically fly into my sister's bookstore, One More Chapter, desperately needing to talk, only to be brought up short when I see two older ladies browsing the murder mystery section.

"Hey," Laken greets, offering us a grin. "Uh oh, what's the matter?" she asks, clearly noticing the look of panic on my face.

I offer her a fake smile and look down at my five-year-old son, Trace. "Why don't you go look at the books."

My mini-me glances at his aunt. "Will you read to me?"

As if anticipating the question, she's already nodding. "Of course I will. Go pick something out and I'll be over to the reading nook in just a few minutes."

"Yay!" he hollers, releasing my hand and practically sprinting toward the children's book section.

"No running!" I whisper-yell, hoping to not disturb the two shoppers quietly discussing the books in their hands.

"What's wrong?" my sister asks quietly as soon as I approach the counter.

Leaning over, I state, "I think I'm about to be fired."

"What? From which job?" she asks, her hazel eyes wide with shock.

I take in my little sister's appearance. Besides having the same eye color, that's about the only similarities we share. While her hair is a gorgeous shade of red, mine is brown and flat. She has the body of a runner, lean and gorgeous, and standing a solid three inches taller than me. I have the hips and butt that makes buying pants more difficult because the sizes that fit my ass are like five inches too long.

And let's not discuss my boobs. They practically need their own zip codes. While they might be the first thing guys notice, resulting in a lot of inappropriate leering, they're nothing but an inconvenience to me. The moment I got pregnant with Trace, they got bigger and never went down, even after I was through breastfeeding. Now, I wear a lot of sports bras, just to try to keep them contained and not appear as big as they are.

I sigh, resting my elbows on the counter. "The City Hall one."

"No," she whines. "You just got that one. What happened?"

I close my eyes, instantly replaying the images I've been unable to forget from last night. When I open them she's staring, waiting on me to explain. "I, uh, might have walked into the bathroom and seen the mayor naked."

Her eyes practically pop out of her head, and if I weren't a nanosecond away from freaking out, I'd find it comical. "Shut. Up. Really? How? When? How?"

"Ugh," I groan loudly, covering my eyes. Of course, the very vivid details of seeing Malcolm Wright standing there in the buff won't subside. They've plagued me since I left the very bathroom I found him standing naked in.

Laken comes around the counter and drags me behind it. "Spill."

"I was cleaning after their meeting, and thought I was alone, like the last few weeks. There were some lights on, but that's happened before. I thought someone just forgot to shut them off. I went into his office and decided to start in the bathroom. The door was slightly ajar, but I didn't hear anything, so I went inside."

I blink, replaying the ultimate humiliation. "He was just getting out of the shower, Lake. He was...naked. And wet," I add with a whisper.

My sister is grinning from ear to ear. "Was it...on display?" she mutters, making sure no one else can hear.

I nod. "Very largely displayed. Like your storefront window during Dr. Suess's birthday celebration."

She giggles. "Oh my God, I can't believe you saw Malcolm naked!"

I groan and glance over to where my son continues to look for the perfect book. "Can we stop talking about it now? I just got that job, and now I'm definitely getting fired."

"Why?"

"Because I just burst into the bathroom without knocking. Lake, I was completely unprofessional too. I mean, I covered my eyes, but...I didn't exactly leave right away."

My traitorous sister covers her mouth to try to hide her laughter. "So, you snuck a few peeks?"

"A lot of peeks. And I'm pretty sure he knew it too."

Now she's fully bent over, laughing so hard, she struggles to catch her breath. "So, let me get this straight. You were busted ogling the mayor in his private bathroom, while he was completely naked, and you were supposed to be cleaning?"

I nod, squeezing my eyes closed to avoid her gaze.

"Oh, I'm sure you're fine, Len. Everyone ogles that man, and besides, you're probably one of the only women in the county who hasn't seen him naked," she replies with a shrug.

Now, my own eyes widen. "Wait. You've..."

She waves off my suggestion. "No, not me. I was being sarcastic. That man gets around. A lot."

So I've heard. It's hard to go anywhere without overhearing someone talking about the sexy mayor. He's the youngest person to ever hold that position in Mason Creek, and even though he's a bit of a playboy, he won the election by a landslide. It may have something to do with the fact his father and grandfather both held the position over the years, and everyone seems to like the Wright family.

"Ugh!" I bellow just as my son runs to the counter.

"Aunt Laken, can you read me this one?" he asks, proudly holding up a book on fishing.

"I'd love to," my sister replies, moving around the counter, taking my son's hand, and leading him back to the nook.

Instead of joining them, I decide to browse her store, looking for my own book to read. I've never been much of a reader, always preferring music and puzzles, but have learned to appreciate a good book as an adult. Of course, there isn't much time for reading when you're a single mom with a young son. However, now that he's five and in kindergarten and doesn't require my constant attention, I find my own time is a little more flexible.

Since the other shoppers are in the murder mystery section, I head for the romance department. There are a few books I recognize from recent announcements, something about books made into movies for a streaming service and can't help but notice the big endcap displays my sister has set up. She's always been a big fan of authors, preferring books over movies, but I imagine having some of her favorites turned into something for the small screen is a big deal, even to her.

One particular cover catches my attention. It features a gorgeous man, his button-down shirt open and his abs on full exhibit. I can't help but recall another set of abs recently on display. They were rippled and hard, much like the rest of his body. Even as he casually threw his towel over his shoulders, I noticed perfectly sculpted arms and tight thighs you could climb like a tree.

I flip the book over and read the blurb on the back. It immediately grabs my attention, talking about a single mom and the playboy she tamed. A snort leaves my mouth, uncontrolled and very unladylike.

"What's funny?"

I jump, not realizing my sister's fiancé had entered the shop and walked up behind me. "Oh, hey, Grayson."

"Hi, Leni. Whatcha reading?" he asks, his green eyes sparkling like emeralds, even under the lower fluorescent lighting.

"Uh," I stammer, holding up the book and blushing a bit at the cover. "I was just looking around."

He smiles, one of those gorgeous smiles that my sister has always found irresistible, even back in high school when she had the ultimate crush on him. "Your sister read that one a few weeks ago. Some of it to me," he mutters with a far-off grin, as if recalling something I probably don't want to know about.

"Where are the girls?" I ask, trying to redirect the conversation. Grayson was a single dad before he got together with my sister. Harlow and Hayden are his four-year-old twin daughters from his first marriage, a union that ended when she unexpectedly passed away when the girls were only a year old.

"They're with my mom. I just got off work, so I thought I'd stop by and steal a kiss from my girl before I go pick them up," he replies.

"Trace will be sad they're not here," I tell him, glancing over to where my sister reads to my son.

Grayson snorts out a laugh. "I bet. Last time they were together, I heard they talked him into painting his toenails."

I can't help but giggle as well. "They were blue, so he thought it was okay because it was a boy color."

"I'm sorry," he mumbles, the softest blush tinting his cheeks as he tries to hide his grin. "They're a lot, especially when they conspire together."

I wave off his apology. "I wasn't worried about it. It came off with nail polish remover."

"Yeah, well, I'd like to apologize anyway. And for all the things they'll do in the future."

A bubble of laughter spills from my mouth. "Well, Trace loves having them around. He says they like getting muddy too, so maybe I need to be apologizing to you."

Before he can reply, the fast footballs of a runner catch our attention. "Mommy, I want to go fishing like Ernie did in the book!" Trace hollers.

"Shh, don't yell inside, remember?"

"Oh, sorry." He turns to my sister and gives her a shy grin. "Thank you for reading to me."

"You're welcome, little man. Come back next week, okay?" she says, noticing the man standing beside me. Oh, who am I kidding? She noticed him right away. "Hey, you."

"We'll get going," I add, nodding toward the front counter, where the two shoppers from earlier are standing to make their purchases.

"Sounds good," my sister replies, though I can tell her attention is already turned to her fiancé as they move to the front of the bookstore.

"Ready to go?" I ask, taking Trace's hand in my own.

"What's for dinner?" he asks as soon as we step out onto the sidewalk and toward my car.

"I think Nana said something about spaghetti and garlic toast."

"Yay!" he proclaims, jumping up and down right where he walks. "I love pasgetti."

Smiling, I unlock my car doors and help him inside. Trace jumps right into his seat and fastens the buckles. "Ready, Freddie?"

My son starts giggling. "I'm not Freddie. I'm Trace!"

"Oh, that's right. I keep forgetting," I tease, closing the door and making my way to the driver's door.

Just before I pull it open, movement down the sidewalk catches my eye. A tall man steps out of Stitches Seamstress carrying a pair of pants. He slides a pair of aviators on his face, his long gait eating up the walkway with ease and confidence. I recognize him instantly.

Malcolm.

I can feel my cheeks instantly heating up, remembering exactly what he's hiding beneath that finely pressed suit. I need to get away before he can see me and be reminded of my voyeurism last night.

Quickly.

I tug on my door handle and step back into the roadway just as a car comes around the corner. The driver honks his horn and swerves into the other lane, thankfully without causing an accident from oncoming traffic.

Plastering myself against my car, I try to calm my racing heart.

"Are you okay?"

I startle and turn fast. Two big, warm hands grab my arms to keep me from stumbling, only to come face to face with the man I was trying to avoid. "Oh, yes. Thanks." I offer him a quick, reassuring grin.

"Are you sure? You almost got flattened by a teenager, who clearly rolled that stop sign," he replies, glaring off in the direction the swiftly moving car went.

I chuckle. "Yes, I'm fine, thank you. I appreciate you keeping me from falling on my face," I add, awkwardly. Glancing down, I realize he dropped the pants he was carrying earlier. "Oh no, your pants are down."

It takes a second before my words register, and when they do, he busts out laughing. "Well, that's better than not wearing them at all, right?" he replies with a wink.

I swear, if it were possible, I'd love for the road to open up and swallow me whole. That's the only way to end this mortification. I cover my mouth with my hands. "That's not...I didn't mean...oh my God!"

Malcolm chuckles and squats down to grab the hanger, leaving one hand still holding my arm. "I know what you meant, Lenora."

"I...can't believe I said that. Or did what I did last night. I'm so sorry, sir."

He smirks. "Just Malcolm. And it's all right," he says leaning forward. "Besides, it's not the first time someone has walked in on me in an undressed state.

Fortunately for me, the last time, Gladys wasn't wearing her bifocals, which was why she didn't realize my bathroom was occupied." He stands up straight and meets my gaze. "But I suspect your vision is much better." He smiles, perfectly straight, white teeth that could probably do wonderfully dirty things to a woman's body.

Kill. Me. Now.

"Again," I start, but he cuts me off.

"I don't want to hear any more apologies. Clearly you didn't mean to," he adds.

There's a knock on the window, and my eyes are drawn down. "I have to go to the bathroom!" Trace hollers through the door. "Bad!" he adds, reaching down and holding himself for good measure.

"I'm so sorry, but I need to go," I state quickly, reaching for the door handle.

Malcolm beats me to it though, pulling open the door and stepping aside. "I have a bathroom at City Hall, if that would help," he says, eyeing the back seat with curiosity.

"Thank you for the offer, but I only live around the corner. We can make it home," I insist, slipping into my car.

As I reach for the door, he pushes it closed. I fire up my car and roll down the window. "It was a pleasure to see you again, Lenora."

"My friends call me Leni," I state, putting my car in drive. "Oh, and I'm very sorry for making you drop your drawers."

My words register.

My God!

"I'm going to stop talking now. Goodbye, Malcolm," I say, as I pull from the parking spot and pull into the street, heading around the square to get back to my place.

Before I turn the corner, however, I glance in the rearview mirror, only to find Malcolm standing in the same place I left him. He doesn't seem concerned that someone could whip around the corner and hit him. He's just standing there, watching me drive away.

A shiver of awareness slips down my spine, but I ignore it.

The last thing I need is to notice someone like Malcolm Wright.

Worse, the last thing I need is someone like Malcolm Wright noticing me.

Not that I have too much to worry about there. I'm a single mom with wide birthing hips and a big ass. I wear yoga pants yet haven't attended one yoga class in my entire life. I clean houses and businesses and own the town laundromat. Hell, I clean *his* family-owned business.

Plus, I often smell like disinfectant and peanut butter and jelly sandwiches.

Grape, not strawberry.

My life isn't my own and won't be until my son turns eighteen.

Believe me, there's nothing exciting or great to look at here.

Chapter THREE

Malcolm

I'm intrigued.

And have no idea why.

As I watch her little Altima drive away, I am overcome with a sense of interest, which still shocks me to the bone. It did last night after she made her hasty escape and I wanted to follow her. It reappeared just a few minutes ago when I looked up and saw her beside her car, about to be run over by that teenage driver.

Clearly, deciding to take the long way around the square to get back to my office was the right decision.

Except, it probably wasn't.

Sure, I may find Leni Abbott attractive, but I shouldn't. She's not my usual type, but also there's the big factor of her son. I've dated a lot of women in my life, but never a single mom like that. Divorcees, yes. Kids go to Dad's for the weekend, and Mom is looking to unwind. That's where I come in.

Then there's the physical differences. The women I've dated in the past are model thin. You know the ones who barely eat a few bites of their salads and proclaim themselves full? I've never understood it, personally, but whatever. Lenora isn't overweight. Not by a long shot. She's got that perfect hourglass figure that drives men wild, me included. All I thought about last night was gripping onto those hips and thrusting into her from behind. It made for an uncomfortable night's sleep.

And morning.

I was determined to forget all about the pretty woman who apparently now cleans City Hall, but then fate dealt me a cruel hand, and minutes ago, I found her again.

At least this time I was wearing pants.

I snicker as I return to the sidewalk, recalling her comments about me dropping my drawers and the look of mortification that appeared on her pretty face moments later. Talk about opening mouth and inserting foot.

Oh, the things I could do with her mouth…

Clearing my throat, I head down the walkway and round the corner, my recently tailored suit pants thrown over my arm. I turn where Plumbing Solutions sits and pass the laundromat in the middle of the block. Something niggles at the back of my mind, and I find myself stopping in the middle of the walkway.

I glance through the windows of Squeaky Clean as realization sets in.

Lenora Abbott owns this place and lives above it. I recall when the previous owner retired a few months back and sold it. I heard mention at one of the Chamber of Commerce gatherings that the woman who bought it had just returned home after being away for several years, and also cleans houses and businesses in town.

My family's law office and City Hall included.

As I keep walking, I realize how incredibly brave it was for this woman to open a business in a town she hasn't lived in for a while. Especially one as young as twenty-nine, six years my junior. But I imagine it gives her a steady income with the flexibility she needs to raise a child alone.

At least I think she's doing it alone.

I've not heard anything about a boyfriend or ex hanging around, and usually all gossip makes its way past my desk at some point.

I worm my way back to City Hall, prepared to put in a few hours of work before the public works committee meeting later this evening. As I pass Shana's desk, I can't help but stop. "Hey, Shana. Can I ask you a question?"

The woman in her mid-forties gives me her full attention, pushing her chair away from her computer desk. "Sure, Mal. What's up?"

"The woman who cleans this place, she's fairly new, right?"

The woman I hired right after taking office nods her head. "She is. Been cleaning three weeks now," she informs, though I already knew that. I signed off on her hiring. "She comes highly recommended by several businesses around the square. Why? Is something wrong?" she asks, a look of worry crossing her face.

"No, of course not. I was just curious. I've been considering having my place cleaned at home every week or so and thought maybe she'd be a good fit."

"Leni's fabulous. She cleans Jim's mom's place, as well as Hazel's sister's neighbor's condo. Heck, she could probably give you a whole list of references around Mason Creek. Everyone uses her."

I nod. "Okay. I'm pretty sure that's who Dad uses at the law office. Do you have a contact for her?"

"I do," she states, pulling open a desk drawer and grabbing a Rolodex. You know, like a good, old fashioned business card holder and contact keeper. "Do you want me to email it to you?" she asks, stopping on a small card with bold lettering across the top.

"No need. I'll just program it into my phone," I say, glancing over her shoulder and inputting her name and cell number into my contacts.

Not that I plan to use it.

"Thanks, Shana."

"You're welcome, Mal. Oh, don't forget, you have that meeting request with Aqua Solutions, the company who manages the water treatment facility. They're still hoping to get in this week."

I sigh, having put off this request for almost a week. I know why they're calling. They want to negotiate new rates for this next contract, and I'm not looking forward to playing hardball with them. The owner is a bastard who tries to cut corners at all costs, including how they monitor our water treatment facility. "I'll email them back shortly. It'll have to be next week, though. My schedule is already full."

It's not.

She knows it.

I know it.

But I'm not in a hurry to deal with them right now.

I slip my phone into my pocket and head to my office, hanging up my trousers on the hook behind my door as I go. I boot up my computer and take a seat, just as my phone vibrates in my pants. A part of me hopes it's Lenora, but then I realize how silly I'm being. She doesn't have my number, and why the hell would she be texting me anyway?

Spying the name on the screen, I sigh. It's Jessa, and there's only one reason she'd be texting me on a Wednesday evening.

Jessa: Hey, darling. I was hoping you'd be free later this evening. It's been too long since I've seen you. *winky face*

That's code for too long since we hooked up. It's probably been about two months since her last text message invitation arrived on my phone, and the last time since I arrived on her doorstep. Jessa Donaldson is a recent divorcee, as well as a widow. When she was in her mid-twenties, she married a wealthy politician old enough to be her grandpa. When he died unexpectedly a few years later, she was left everything in his name, including vacation houses and a stake in a transportation company.

Then, she moved on to another older man, though the second one only about twenty years her senior. When he found out she was sleeping with everyone and their brother—including his own brother—he filed for divorce. Unfortunately for him, he didn't have a prenup, so he had to give half his net worth to his cheating wife. She walked away with a cool 7.5 million bucks and relocated to the biggest estate in Mason Creek.

I met Jessa a year ago when she showed up at our law firm to meet with my dad. Later that night, I was balls-deep between her thighs and we've had a casual arrangement ever since. No commitment. No relationship. No strings.

Sex.

Whenever, wherever.

My finger lingers over her message, trying to figure out how to reply. Do I want to meet up with Jessa later? My dick says yes, but my head tells me I'm busy and it's not a good time. I have a committee meeting later, plus some paperwork on a new custody case that landed on my desk I need to review.

Me: Sorry, doll. Busy. Another time.

I can almost hear her pout all the way across town.

Jessa: You know you can drop by anytime. I'm always available for you.

Me: I do know that, but I have meetings.

Jessa: Tomorrow then. I have an appointment with my cosmetologist to get things waxed.

I almost groan. Jessa's a fan of going bare and not afraid to show it.

Me: Maybe another time.

Jessa: Fine. I suppose I could find someone else to entertain...

She's used jealousy on me before, but it's not going to work this time. In the very beginning, she mentioned someone else, and I went running with my tongue hanging out, like she knew I would. Now, I don't even feel a bubble of envy or anything at the thought of her hooking up with someone besides me. I've known all along I'm not her only friend, and that's never bothered me much. Still doesn't.

We just don't have that kind of relationship. When I'm seeing someone else, I don't respond to Jessa. Even if I don't do the whole long-term dating thing, I'm still a one-woman man. We're casual, and that's all.

Me: Have a good night, Jessa.

I click off the texting app and set my phone down, ignoring the alerts of messages that follow. Instead, I focus on my work and prepping for the meeting later. Of course, my thoughts are still invaded by a sexy brunette with alluring hazel eyes. I picture her shocked expression last night when she found me standing naked in the bathroom and the stunned look on her face when I kept her from falling today. As much as I try to push all thoughts of her aside, I can't. I'm intrigued, and I don't know why. I've never been so curious about a woman, especially one with a young kid, but here I am, wondering what she's doing tonight. Is she working? At home with her son? Out on a date?

And why does that last one bother me so much?

"How'd the meeting go?" my dad asks when he answers the phone.

"Fine. We prioritized a list of roads that we'll repair this year. Six are considered top priority, with another four to be done next fiscal year."

"Good," he replies, knowing what it's like to prioritize projects based on the budget. "That's a start. I know there are several that need some patch work too."

"That and pipe work. We're going to have to upgrade the water pipes for the entire south side of town within the next four to five years. We're looking into grants and bond options."

"That sounds like a solid plan." Dad takes a drink from a glass, most likely scotch. It's part of his nightly routine after a long day in court. "So, why did you call me after nine? Not that I care, because you know I'm still up, but I'm sure it wasn't to discuss the public works committee meeting."

"I've been thinking," I start as I drive through the streets, heading for home, but don't finish my sentence.

"About?"

"I'm thinking of hiring a cleaning service. For the house."

I'm met with silence on the other end of the line. It drags on for so long, I check the screen on my dashboard to make sure we didn't lose our connection. After what feels like the world's longest pause, he finally says, "Okay? You work a lot of hours, so a cleaning service would probably be beneficial."

"Yeah, yeah. I thought so too." *This is going swimmingly well*, I think to myself as I reach my driveway and press the button to raise the garage door.

"Malcolm, what is it you want to know?"

"How well do you know the woman who cleans the office for us?" I ask, parking my car in my garage and lowering the door. Once it's down, I turn off my car, but leave it in accessory so I can keep the Bluetooth connected.

"Not super well, but I've heard a lot about her. She cleans Debi's house, and she recommended her," he says, referring to our office manager. "She seems very professional and efficient. I know the Abbotts, Lisa and Lewis. Lived in town as long as our family has. Plus, your mother loves that bookstore the younger daughter owns. Spends all my money there." He snickers at his comment, even though I'm sure that's not true.

"You'll make more," I tease.

Dad barks out a laugh. "That I will. Now, something tells me that's not the real reason you were asking about the Abbott girl, is it?"

I sigh, turn off the car, and put my cell phone to my ear. My long legs carry me into my laundry room, where I kick off my shoes. "I met her in an official capacity last night." I leave out the part about how. "She was...fascinating."

I can practically hear him thinking, and before I can tell him not to look too much into my words, he replies, "I hear she has a son."

My throat is dry. "Yeah."

"Well, I think if you need to be careful if you hire her. You don't want to give her a job and then do something that causes her to quit."

I read his unspoken insinuation loud and clear. He's telling me not to sleep with her after I hire her to clean my house. She has a son to take care of, and if I'm just going to hump and dump her, I better think twice.

But the truth is, no matter how much I want to hump, I can tell it's more than that. I've never been this captivated by a woman. Ever.

That's exactly why there will be no humping.

I'll offer her a job, cleaning my house, and that's it. End of story.

"You're right, Dad. Thanks."

His low chuckle accompanies me into my kitchen. "Well, I'm not saying you shouldn't be interested. I'm saying you need to be careful if you are."

"I'm always careful," I state, grabbing a glass from the cabinet.

He snorts a laugh. "I'm sure you are," he replies dryly. "Anyway, I should get back to this deposition. Why don't you come over later in the week for dinner? Your mom will cook."

"Sounds good. I could use a good homecooked meal." Surprisingly, my mom is great in the kitchen, considering she grew up with a small staff in their house to help with the day-to-day aspects.

"She's come a long way since those early days of burnt dinners and failed meal plans. There were a lot of tears the first few years of our marriage, but that's one of the things I love the most about your mother. She's resilient and won't stop until she accomplishes her task," my dad replies quietly.

"I know. She's the best." And she is. My mom stayed home with me but would never trust my care to a nanny like her parents insisted. She wanted to do it herself and was hands-on my entire childhood.

"We'll see you in the office tomorrow?"

"I'll be there."

"Goodnight, Malcolm."

"Night, Dad."

When we hang up, I mentally run through tomorrow's schedule. I have a few cases to work on in the morning, but I'll be back at City Hall in the afternoon. And maybe I'll make a phone call. I mean, my house is probably dusty, and my dirty dishes are definitely piled up. It would definitely help to have someone who keeps this place clean, right? And if the woman who does it happens to be a stunning, beautiful woman?

That's just a bonus.

What's a single guy to do?

Chapter
FOUR

Leni

I'm just wrapping up at the Gomez house when my cell rings. It's not a number I recognize, and while I'd prefer to let it go to voicemail, when you own a business, you don't always have the luxury. Every missed call could be a missed opportunity, or so my mom used to say when I was first starting out.

I make sure I have all of my cleaning supplies gathered up before answering the phone. "Squeaky Clean, this is Leni."

"Lenora."

That's all the caller says, but I know instantly who it is. The deep timbre of his voice, raspy and seductive, has my thighs clenching by saying just one word.

My name.

"It's Leni," I tell him, trying to control my breathing.

Malcolm chuckles. "I prefer Lenora. It's exotic, don't you think?"

I feel my internal muscles spasm as his voice dips down, as if he's sharing a dirty secret. Clearing my throat, and the dirty images suddenly flashing through my mind, I stand up straight, refusing to let him get to me. "It's old-fashioned and the reason I was teased in grade school," I retort, though I instantly wish I wouldn't have said a word. That's none of his business, really.

He tsks. "That's unfortunate. Kids are cruel, that's for sure. I find the name unique and interesting."

"Anyway, what can I do for you, Mr. Mayor?"

"Ahh, I see you already know who this is. Keeping tabs on me?" he teases with a low snicker that sends my blood pumping.

"No, but I recognized your voice."

"All right, well, I was hoping to hire you."

I grab my bag and pull out my calendar, preferring the paper version over a digital one. "What kind of job? I already clean the public building and the law firm."

"It's a personal one." Before I can reply, he takes control over the conversation. "Do you have time to meet with me? Say this afternoon? Two o'clock?"

Scanning today's schedule, I actually have a big hole with availability because my evening is packed. "That should be fine."

"Two it is. I'll text you my address," he informs, before adding, "See you later, Lenora."

"Thank you, sir."

"It's Malcolm, Lenora," he replies before signing off.

I jot his name down into my schedule and try to calm my racing heart. I'm not sure what it is about this man that causes me to get all mushy and silly, like a schoolgirl with a crush.

My phone chimes with a text message, so I quickly add his address beneath his name, and while I should just finish packing up my things, I take a few seconds to add his contact to my phone.

Not like I'll ever use it, though.

I return the supplies provided by the homeowner to the closet and stick my products back into my carrying tote. While I may use a client's broom and mop, I prefer my own cleaning products. They're made of all-natural ingredients, smell amazing, and are simply the best on the market. There are a few that request I use their cleaners, usually laden with harsh chemicals and horrible odors, but fortunately, those clients are few and far in between.

I also sell this particular product line through the laundromat. On Monday evenings from four to six and Thursday mornings from nine to eleven, people can stop in and purchase the same supplies I use for their own homes. It's actually been a great opportunity for me, as well as the residents of Mason Creek.

After loading up my car at the Gomez house and resetting their alarm, I make my way back to my storefront and try not to fret about the impending meeting with Malcolm.

Yeah, fat chance of that happening.

At five 'til two, I pull into the driveway of a gorgeous house. It's one of the newer ones in town, built during my time away from Mason Creek. It's a two-story brick home, with gorgeous landscaping and a two-car attached garage. The others in the subdivision are of similar size and style, with large yards. Some have visible swing sets in the backyards, while others have basketball hoops in the driveway, Malcolm's included.

I get out of my car and grab my bag, making sure I have my notebook and planner, and head for the front door. It opens before I even reach the concrete steps, and the man I've been nervous to see again steps out. "Welcome, Lenora."

"Hi," I chirp, adjusting the shoulder strap on my bag to give me something to do.

"Won't you come in?" he offers, stepping aside and holding the screened door wide open for me to enter.

The foyer is bright and professionally decorated, with a side table and fancy decorative bowl that probably costs more than my entire outfit.

"Come on in," he adds, waving me down a small hallway and into the kitchen.

I glance around, taking in the cabinets and appliances, the rich sage walls, and a table big enough to seat eight. But what really catches my attention is the view. I set my bag down on the counter and move to the large bay window overlooking Baylor Lake. I can see families outside, fishing and swimming in the warm summer sun, and dogs splashing in the water.

Malcolm's backyard is massive, much bigger than the neighbors, with a decent-sized shed positioned on the far-left side of the property line, so it doesn't obstruct the view of the waterfront.

Wow, being mayor and an attorney, even one who's only thirty-five, must be lucrative.

"This view is amazing," I state, though I'm sure he already knows.

"It was one of the reasons I purchased this house. I grew up swimming in Baylor Lake as a child and love to fish."

I glance over my shoulder, realizing he's standing directly behind me, gazing out at the view. I catch a whiff of his cologne, the scent woodsy and clean and doing a number on my lady bits. Clearing all thoughts of my unused *parts* from my mind, I return my focus back to our conversation. "My son has been talking about fishing. My dad took him a few months back, after we moved home. He's been wanting to go again ever since."

He shoves his hands into his pockets and turns his milk chocolate gaze my way. "You're welcome to bring him here."

"Oh, that's okay," I reply quickly, waving off his invitation. I barely know this man. "Thank you, though."

He shrugs. "The offer stands anytime. I rarely get out there and fish anymore, but I have poles and supplies in the storage shed. You're welcome to bring your son and use them."

I reply with a grin and turn back to collect my bag. I retrieve my planner, pen, and notebook, ready to make notes if needed. "So, what is it you need help with?"

He waves at the chair closest to me and takes the one directly across the table. "I'm looking for someone to clean my place. I'd do it myself, but with my schedule, it can be hard to keep up with it. What sort of services do you offer?"

I pull out a printed price list, complete with three package options. "These are my services. They're based on a bi-weekly schedule, though some prefer weekly. If that's the case, most choose a deeper clean on the odd weeks, with the basic package on the evens."

"I'll do that."

I blink rapidly at his quick decision. He didn't even look at the print-out long enough to see the package differences. "Oh. Okay. You don't want to take more time to look this over and make a decision?"

He shrugs again and crosses his arms over his chest. Even with the light blue button-down shirt, I can see the chiseled muscles of his upper arms through the material. My mouth goes dry. "No need. You come highly recommended by pretty much everyone in this town."

"Oh. Well, thank you. I appreciate their vote of confidence."

"When are you free? How soon can you start?" he asks, pulling out his cell phone. I see his long fingers tapping away, pulling up the calendar app.

"Well, I guess we need to discuss your needs." I glance up and see his eyes turn molten. It causes me to lose all train of thought.

After a few long seconds, the corner of his mouth turns heavenward as he asks, "We were about to discuss my needs."

The innuendo isn't lost on me, and I'm sure he can tell by the way my breathing hitches in my throat. "Yes, of course," I mumble, glancing down at my notebook. "Are there any particular days and times you prefer?"

"Not really."

"Well, if you prefer to be here while I clean," I start, glancing at my schedule.

"What do most do?"

"I have clients who are here while I work and others who provide me with a key or security code to gain entrance."

He seems to consider both options. "What do you do with your son while you work?"

His question catches me a little off guard, but not entirely. It's no secret I have a child, and it can be a challenge to coordinate his schedule with that of a homeowner's. Since he's out of school for the summer, I'm a little more flexible, since he stays with my mom while I work. Once school starts in a few weeks, I'll have to adjust my schedule so I can pick him up at the end of the day. Sure, I can have my mom help, but it's something I'm looking forward to doing. I want to be there when Trace gets out of school, listen to him tell me all about his day in kindergarten, and preparing him an after-school snack. That's part of the reason I chose this field of work.

Flexibility.

Well, that and I love to clean.

I meet Malcolm's gaze to answer his question. "He stays with my mom while I work, sometimes my sister. I try to limit the nights I clean to three, so I can be home with him in the evenings."

He nods, seeming to consider my words. "Do you ever bring him with you?"

I'm sure my surprise is evident. "I try not to. He's five, and sometimes that's not conducive to the whole cleaning process." I give him a smile, which makes him grin in return.

"I bet not. I guess I'm just saying, if you ever need to bring him, you're welcome to," he says with a casual shoulder lift.

"Oh, well, thank you. I hope I shouldn't need to."

"Anyway, let's figure out a schedule that works for both of us. How does Thursday evenings sound?"

I glance down, noticing I have availability on Thursdays. "I can fit you in after the physician's office. I'm usually done by seven."

"Okay. That works for me. I don't have committee meetings on Thursdays, so it's a great night for me. I'll also get you a security code number for the front door. This way, if I'm not here for some reason, you'll have access."

I make a few notes in my binder. "We can begin with the basic clean. When do you want to start?"

"How about this week?"

My eyes widen slightly. "Tomorrow?"

"The sooner, the better, right?"

"Of course," I insist, penciling Malcolm into tomorrow's schedule and the next few Thursdays after that.

We spend the next few minutes going over the details of the contract, and I'm grateful Malcolm chooses to use the products I sell. I think he'll really be happy with the results. By the time he signs on the dotted line, it's getting close to my next appointment.

"If you don't have any more questions, I'll see you tomorrow just after seven then," I state, standing and gathering my belongings.

"Perfect," he replies, rising and waiting to escort me to the door. "I look forward to working with you, Lenora."

I glance briefly at his offered hand. When he takes mine and our palms touch, a bolt of electricity zips through my veins, alive and unfamiliar. The shock has me pulling mine from his grasp, but it does nothing to ebb the power of that touch. "Tomorrow," I mumble, stepping toward the door, ready to make my escape.

Malcolm is there, holding the door open. "I'll see you soon."

I slip past him, catching that now-familiar woodsy scent of his cologne as I go, and hightail it to my car, needing to get as far away from Malcolm's potent gaze and intoxicating scent. I need to put him far out of my mind. He's a job, a client. Plus, he has a reputation for being a playboy, and I have no time or energy for one of those in my life.

Pulling out of his driveway, I can't help but take a look around. This is the type of place I'd love to raise Trace, but right now, that's not in the cards. I used my inheritance from my grandmother to start my business. Part of what attracted me to the laundromat, besides the income it provided, was the apartment upstairs. My sister Laken did the same thing, and it was such a solid investment. I followed suit.

My ideal job wasn't exactly owning and operating a laundromat. In fact, I actually have a bachelor's degree in accounting from Washington State. I excelled in math all through school and thought a career with numbers was my ticket to financial success. Turns out, I hated it.

I was hired directly out of college to work at a small firm in the city I was living in, and it was horrible. I stuck it out for a few years, at the advice of my mom, especially since I was pregnant at twenty-three. With a baby on the way and a boyfriend who traveled for his job, I needed steady employment. So I stayed, hating my job, until the day I left Washington and returned home to Montana.

Now I'm the proud owner of an aging laundromat, who spends her weekend cleaning a cheap disposable diaper out of a washing machine. Did you know they swell up and explode all over the place when put in the spin cycle?

This is the life, isn't it?

Sighing, I head to my next appointment, an old man who cooks bacon three times a day and tries to give me a smooshed Tootsie Roll from his pocket when I leave. At least I get to look forward to spending twenty minutes scrubbing splattered grease off the range, the counter, and the walls. Hell, it'll even be all over the floor, especially knowing he likely stepped in it and dragged it all over the faded linoleum.

Yes, this is the life.

My life.

And I'm loving every second of it.

Chapter FIVE

Malcolm

I work quickly through the day, anxious to go home. I've never been one to speed through my job, but here I am, driving home after work to meet Lenora. It's just before six, which gives me time for a short run and shower before she arrives.

My feet pound the pavement as I head out of town. There's plenty of light to be seen on the country roads, and it gets me away from the insistent waves and flirty smiles I usually receive on my in-town route. I can feel my phone vibrate in my pocket, but I ignore it. I already know who it is. She's been texting all day, hoping to drop by for a visit. The problem is Jessa is well aware of my meeting schedule, and even though I told her I had a prior obligation tonight, she's relentless.

My run takes just over forty minutes, and by the time I return to my house, I know it's getting close to seeing Lenora. Leni. She looks like a Leni, cute with a hint of a shy personality. However, there's an added danger value I'm attracted to when I use her full name. She's not a fan of her full name, but there's no denying the way her eyes dilate and her breath hitches when I use it.

It's sexy as hell.

The shower I take is on the faster side, but I tell myself it's because I don't want to be standing here naked when she arrives. Reality of that prospect doesn't bother me one bit. In fact, it excites me. A little too much, if you know what I mean. The truth is, I want to be ready and waiting downstairs when she arrives. To help her with anything she may need to carry in.

I'm a gentleman like that.

Lenora pulls in at almost seven on the dot and starts unloading a plastic tote and a carrying bag with supplies. I meet her on the sidewalk and reach for the handle of the rolling tote. "I can get it," she states, giving me a small smile as she walks by.

My eyes are immediately drawn down to her ass in black yoga capris. An ass that's like the whipped cream on my hot fudge sundae it's that fucking fabulous.

She steps through the open door, carefully lifting the plastic tote over the threshold, and never once asks for help. All I can do is stand there and watch, completely drawn to her drive, her tenacity, and her spunk, as well as her ass.

"Before I begin, is there anywhere you don't want me to go? Any room I shouldn't clean?"

I arch an eyebrow. "Like?"

She shrugs, pulling out her supplies and arranging them on the kitchen floor. "An office? Bedroom? Den? Possible sex cave with questionable items mounted to the walls?"

My eyes must bug out of my head. "A what? You've had a client with that?"

She meets my gaze and chuckles. "Well, no, not me, but someone recently in one of the chatrooms I belong to had that happen. She walked into something right out of that *Fifty Shades of Grey* movie." Lenora stands up, a microfiber cloth and spray bottle in her hands. "The worst I've ever found is a few dirty movies and what I assume was a very large butt plug." She shrugs her shoulders, as if it's no big deal, and heads for the staircase. "Mind if I start upstairs?"

I stand there in stunned silence, waving off her question. I focus on the sound of her tennis shoes walking up the hardwood steps and try to wrap my head around what she just said. Just before she reaches the second floor, I can't help but ask, "Who?"

Her bubble of laughter filters down to where I stand. "Not telling."

Then, she's gone, getting to work cleaning my upstairs. Is it wrong that a part of me hopes she's walking into my bedroom right now?

I stay in my kitchen for about fifteen minutes, drinking water and scanning some documents from work, but my mind is elsewhere. Finally, unable to stand it any longer, I swipe my water bottle off the table and move toward the stairs. When I reach the second story, I find Lenora in my guest room. "How's it going?" I ask, leaning against the doorjamb.

"Oh," she startles, turning to face me. "Well. I've got the two bathrooms done and just starting on this room." She turns back around and finishes dusting the nightstand before moving to the dresser.

"How long does it take? To clean?"

She looks around for a second. "A house this size? Two hours for a basic clean, three to four for the deeper one."

I nod, watching her work. It probably stated that on the information sheet she presented me, but I didn't really look at it. "That's a pretty late evening," I observe, my eyes following her movements around the guest room.

She shrugs but keeps working. "It can be. That's why I try to stick with only three nights, sometimes four."

"What about your son?" I finally ask, finding myself wildly curious about the little boy with dark brown hair and the same hazel eyes as his mother.

Lenora meets my gaze once more. "He's with my sister tonight having a sleepover with Grayson's twins." She goes about her business.

I don't know why, but that makes me feel a little better about keeping her away so late on a random Thursday. Yet, I can't stop this really foreign emotion that keeps niggling at me.

Guilt.

"What's his name?" I ask, genuinely interested in more details about her personal life.

She stops her cleaning, giving me her full attention again. "Trace. His name is Trace."

I nod, thinking about the little guy strapped into the back seat of Lenora's car and his wide, curious eyes as he hollered at his mom. Why the hell am I thinking so much about Lenora and Trace? I have no clue, but it's oddly...settling, when I usually find it unsettling. I push off the doorframe. "Well, I should let you get back to it. I'll be in my office if you need me."

I turn and hightail it from the room, desperately seeking a little solitude. When I reach my office, I go to close the door, only to realize I want to be able to hear her moving around the house. I tell myself it's because she's working and new to my home, so she might have questions.

But even I'm not buying that load of crap.

The truth is, I like having her here.

As unnerving as that realization is, I roll with it.

For now.

After spending time in my office and getting absolutely nothing done, I made my way to the kitchen and read a newspaper on my tablet. My stomach growls, but to be honest, I've never seen the kitchen shine as much as it does right now, and the last thing I want to do is get breadcrumbs all over the place while making a sandwich.

At almost exactly nine, Lenora comes around the corner carrying her supplies and a beaming smile full of pride. "All done."

"This place looks amazing," I tell her, setting my tablet aside and rising from the table.

She secures all of her product in the plastic tote. "Thanks. You know, your home is fairly clean already. You could probably get away with an every other week schedule," she states as she finishes packing.

If it were any other woman, I might take her up on the offer, but not now. Not when I look forward to having her here as much as I do, especially since I rarely allow ladies I entertain into my space. I'm more of a go to their place kind of man. Much easier to make my exit that way.

"I think I prefer weekly, at least for now," I tell her, trying to act all casual and like the thought of not seeing her every week isn't a little dreadful.

She shrugs as she throws her bag over her shoulder and grabs the handle of her tote on wheels. "Okay, suit yourself. If you ever want to change it, just let me know. Same time next week?"

"If that works for you," I reply, shoving my hands into my pockets to keep from reaching for her.

She smiles, making my heart do this weird skipping motion in my chest. "I'll see you next Thursday." I swear a blush creeps up her neck as she diverts her eyes.

"I look forward to it," I confirm, knowing I one-hundred-percent do. The only problem is that's a whole week away, and that won't do. I'm going to need to see her before then.

Following her out of the kitchen, I slip around her to open the door. She bobbles the tote as she pulls it over the threshold, the plastic container on wheels dropping awkwardly onto the concrete porch.

"Hey, listen, do you want to grab a bite to eat?"

She stops, turning wide hazel eyes my way. "What?"

"Well, it's getting late, and I haven't eaten dinner yet. I'm assuming you haven't either, since you've had a couple of jobs tonight. There's not a whole lot left open this time of night, but we could probably still grab a pizza from Sauce It Up or some nachos from the bar."

I seem to have stunned her by my invitation, and I have to be honest, it's a little unnerving. Most women jump instantly, practically throwing their panties at me before we figure out where we're going. But not Lenora. She seems nervous, shocked, and slightly confused by my offer, and frankly, it's cute as hell.

Lenora glances down at her capri leggings and T-shirt with Squeaky Clean printed across the chest. "Oh, uh, thank you for the offer, but I'm not exactly dressed for dinner. I'll just grab something at home," she reasons, pulling her supplies toward her car once more.

"You look great," I insist. Better than great, actually, but I don't want to scare her off with talk about how amazing her ass looks in those tight leggings or how I want to peel that shirt off her body with my teeth. I'll just keep those little fantasies to myself.

For now.

"Really, but if you're concerned, we can go to Pony Up. They have the best nachos in the entire state of Montana."

She stops at the trunk of her car, looks my way, and arches and eyebrow. "You've had the nachos from there?"

"Of course. Who hasn't?"

She seems shocked I'd eat bar food on a random Thursday night, when the truth is I'd rather eat there than at the fanciest of restaurants. I choose steakhouses or Italian places because it's usually what my date expects, and truthfully, the food doesn't really matter much to me. It's what happens after the meal that I look forward to the most.

However, that's not on my agenda tonight.

Oh, I've thought about it.

A lot.

But it's not the reason I've asked Leni to join me for a meal. She's been working all damn day, busting her ass to support herself and her son, and surely, she's tired. Trace is with his aunt for the night, which means she's got a little free time to enjoy a quiet dinner, where she doesn't have to worry about anyone but herself.

Well, as quiet as you can get at Pony Up.

"Umm," she hems and haws, probably trying to come up with a good excuse to decline.

But I won't let her.

"Just a quick dinner and maybe a beer. You did such an amazing job in the kitchen, I can't stand the thought of getting it dirty yet. You can drive yourself and head home right after. I promise, I won't try anything," I say, leaning in and adding, "unless you want me to."

I throw her a wink and smirk just for good measure.

She laughs nervously before reaching down and lifting the tote into the trunk of her car. As she sets the bag inside, she glances my way and says, "I haven't had their cheeseburger in forever. It does sound good."

I mentally throw my fists up into the air. "Great. Let me go inside and lock up, and I'll meet you there."

She glances down at her appearance once more. "If you're sure," she mutters, not appearing as confident and excited as I am.

"Definitely. Be right back."

I fly inside and grab my keys and wallet off the counter, double-check the back sliding glass door, and secure the front door on my way. After entering the code into the keypad beside the garage door, I jump into my car as soon as the door is up. Fortunately, Lenora is just now backing out of the driveway, so I have plenty of time to catch up to her and make sure she doesn't change her mind.

I pray she doesn't, because I don't remember the last time I was this excited to go to Pony Up, nor can I ignore the reason why.

Chapter SIX

Leni

What am I doing?

I should be heading home for the night, enjoy getting a full night's sleep and not having to wake up at five in the morning because that's what time Trace thinks the good cartoons come on. Instead, I'm pulling into the parking lot near Pony Up and parking in the first available space.

To meet Malcolm.

Malcolm Wright.

The mayor.

Rumor has it he's dated pretty much every single lady in the state of Montana, with no signs of settling down anytime soon.

He's the last man I need to sit down and share a meal with.

A knock on my window startles me. I glance over to find Malcolm standing there, a sheepish grin on his face. Man, he's handsome. I can see why every woman in town loses their mind when he grins. He's charismatic and incredibly personable, which is probably why he was so easily elected mayor.

I open the door and grab my wristlet, meeting him at the side of my car. "Ready?" he asks, standing closely, but not so close it weirds you out or you feel the need to step back. Not like some of the bars I visited with friends back in Washington. I always felt like the single male patrons didn't respect personal space after getting a few drinks in their system.

"Yes."

He flashes me the full wattage of his smile as we slowly make our way to the bar. "You sure? You seemed a little uncertain back there."

I nod. When we reach the door, Malcolm reaches for the handle and pulls the heavy wood. The sound of laughter and country music greets us, and like every time a door opens, everyone turns around to see who has entered.

That's one of the things I didn't miss about this small town.

Jack's behind the bar and waves before filling another drink order for someone sitting at the bar.

"Malcolm!" someone of the female variety hollers from the bar, but I keep my gaze down, trying not to make eye contact.

I feel Malcolm's warm hand press against my lower back, the heat searing my skin through my T-shirt. "How about that table?" he whispers just loud enough to hear above the noise.

"Okay."

He guides me to the table and waits until I sit before taking the chair directly across from me. Just as we get situated, someone comes over to our table. I've seen her around town, but don't know the waitress well. "Hey, Malcolm. Been a while since we've seen you in here," Josie coos without even offering a glance in my direction.

"It has," he replies. "We'd like to get some food, if you've still got the grill going."

"Anything for you," she gushes so sweetly, it makes my teeth ache.

I mentally roll my eyes, only to hear the man across from me chuckle. When I glance up, he's smiling, his dark brown eyes dancing with delight. That's also when I realize that eye roll may not have actually been mental.

Oh well.

"Lenora, what would you like to drink?" he asks, still grinning from ear to ear.

"Just an ice water, please," I reply, glancing up at the woman drooling all over the man sitting across from me. She's still not paying an ounce of attention to me.

"And you, Mr. Mayor?" The way she says it, all breathless and pleasurable, I'm positive she might have just had an orgasm.

"I'll take a Miller Lite draft."

"I'll run and grab your drinks and then get your order," she says, yet makes no move to leave our table.

Finally, when things take a turn toward awkward, the young server turns and moves toward the bar, her hips swinging dramatically as she goes.

"You don't want a drink?" he asks, leaning back and observing me. His gaze feels more like a caress.

"No thank you. I'm driving."

He continues to study me before nodding. "You don't live that far, right?"

Shaking my head, I reply, "No. Trace and I live in the apartment above the laundromat."

Before he can continue, the server returns to fawn all over Malcolm again. She sets down his beer first before scooting a water glass toward me, all while keeping a smile plastered on her lips and her eyes focused on him. In fact, I'm pretty sure she added a layer of lipstick since she left our table a few minutes ago.

Worse, I don't know why her interest bothers me so much.

I tell myself it's because it's just annoying, which it is. I'm pretty sure she couldn't pick me out of a lineup, but Malcolm, she'd have no problem, even if she was blindfolded. But the truth is, there's something about the fact she doesn't even care that he's sitting with me. She's openly flirting with him right in front of me, as if I weren't here.

What if we were dating? Not that we are or ever would but humor me here. She clearly doesn't care I'm here, her attention solely focused on Malcolm. Yes, he's gorgeous. Sexy, even. He has a smile that would make a nun throw away the habit and the richest chocolate brown eyes you could get lost in. He's charismatic and when his attention is on you, he has a way of making you feel like you're the only woman on the planet. So while I get her response, that doesn't mean it's right.

It's women like this that give all women a bad name.

"Lenora?" I startle a bit when he says my name. "Would you like to order?"

"Oh, yeah. Just a cheeseburger for me. Ketchup only."

"Fries?"

I know I should decline, especially since I've been trying to lose a few pounds, but fries are my weakness. Especially when you have a five-year-old whose diet consists of macaroni and cheese, burgers and fries, and cereal. "Yes, please."

I swear she glances down at my body and smirks. "And for you?" Josie coos at Malcolm, returning her full attention to him.

"Burger and fries for me too."

After jotting down the orders on her pad of paper, she pops a hip out and places her hand on his forearm. "Coming right now."

I sigh, looking down, completely uncomfortable with the situation. I knew this was a bad idea. I mean, I know we're just having dinner, but is it too much to ask to not feel like the third wheel at the table? Not that I care. Really. He's a single guy with a reputation that precedes him. He's free to flirt with whoever he wants.

"Sorry about that," he whispers, drawing my attention up from the tabletop.

I paint on a bright smile and lift my shoulders. "Not your fault," I reply automatically, reaching for my water and taking a healthy drink.

He exhales deeply and opens his mouth, as if he's going to say something, but doesn't. Malcolm lifts his own glass and drinks, and even though I try not to, my eyes fix on the way his throat moves while he drinks.

"So," he starts, leaning back in his chair and giving me his full attention, "you left Mason Creek for a while, right? Where'd ya go?"

"Washington," I reply.

"Did you always want to own a business?"

I snort. "Uh, no. I actually went to school for accounting."

His eyes brighten. "Really?"

"Surprising, isn't it? But I was always good at math and accounting seemed like a solid, stable career. Turns out, it's horribly boring and monotonous. It wasn't for me."

"That's when you started your business?" he asks, seeming completely oblivious to the women in the room who are doing everything they can to catch his eye. His attentiveness is all on me.

"Not really. When I lived in Washington, I had Trace to think about. I needed the financial stability of my job to make sure he always had a roof over his head and food in his belly."

I can tell he's processing the information and working through it in his mind. "And his father?" he finally asks, taking a big drink from his glass.

"In and out of our lives when it suited him," I reply bluntly, always hating to talk about Greg and our rocky relationship.

"I'm sorry to hear that," he states, and by the look in his eyes, I can tell he means it. I may not know this man, but I get the impression he only says what he means, whether you want to hear it or not.

"It's okay. I returned home about six months ago, and it's better this way. Trace has gotten to know his grandparents and my sister better than he ever would have if we were still in Washington. Plus, Grayson and his twin girls. He's been amazing with Trace, as if he's always been a part of his family."

"Grayson's a great man. He was several years younger than me in school, but as adults, we have mutual friends."

"He is. My sister adores him."

Our food arrives, and when Malcolm doesn't pay our server a second of attention after a brief thank-you, she flits away without saying another word. I pile the ketchup on my burger and dive right in, starving after not eating much throughout the day.

Our conversation remains fairly easy throughout the meal, and once he finishes his beer, he switches to water. For a woman who doesn't open up to many, I seem to be a little loose-lipped when it comes to the man across from me, and I have no idea why.

He's completely the opposite of pretty much everyone I've ever dated. I've always been attracted to the blue-collar guys with grease or dirt under their fingernails. Guys who work with their hands instead of pushing pencils in an office somewhere. Yet, here I am, practically confessing my life's story to a man wearing an Oxford shirt and imported leather loafers.

I know this because I picked a pair up off his bathroom floor and noticed the handstitched tag.

What is it about Malcolm Wright that I'm attracted to? Besides the fact he's drop-dead gorgeous, because...duh. He's the type of pretty they write romance novels about. Dark eyes, dark lashes, strong, stubbled jaw, and a body that a blind woman would appreciate. He's charming. Probably too much so, actually, and he knows it. He knows every woman—single or married—wants to see him in his boxer briefs. I know this because they were on the bathroom floor too.

Hell, if I was married, even I'd take a moment to appreciate the view.

"How's your food?" he asks, most of his cheeseburger already gone.

"Really good. I don't know why their burgers are so dang good," I inform, dipping my fries into the glob of ketchup two at a time.

"It's the extra grease in the kitchen. If I'm watching a game here with friends, I always get the nachos. It's just canned cheese, but it's good. Like when you go to the ballpark."

My eyebrows draw together. "You're a baseball fan?"

"Played all four years for Mason Creek High. I root for Seattle but have never been to a game at T-Mobile Park. I hope to rectify that someday," he says after taking his final bite of his burger and moving on to his fries.

"Trace and I went to a Mariners game last summer. My firm would get tickets a few times a season."

"I'm completely jealous. How'd he do?" he asks, polishing off his fries before pushing his plate away.

"Not bad. A jumbo pretzel with cheese and cotton candy helped. He passed out in his seat by the seventh inning and had to be carried out of there."

He laughs, a deep, rich sound that makes my blood zing through my veins. "I almost had to be carried out of a Cubs game in college, but for a whole different reason," he replies with a wink. "My roommate was from Chicago, so I went home with him a few times and we'd catch a game. Either Cubs, Bulls, or Blackhawks, depending on the season."

I finish off my own fries just as my phone chimes with a notification. I pull it from my little wristlet to make sure it's not regarding Trace. The last thing I'd want to do is ignore a message if he's sick or hurt. That's one of my biggest fears as a single parent, so even though it's rude to check your phone on a date, I do it anyway.

Wait.

Not a date.

Trying to keep myself from overanalyzing tonight—again—I say, "Do you mind if I check this?"

"Of course not," he replies instantly. "It could be about your son."

I flash him a quick grin before typing in my security code and pulling up the message app and tap on my sister's name.

Laken: YOU'RE ON A DATE WITH THE MAYOR?!?!?!?!?!?!?

My face flushes a deep red, I know it. I can feel the burn of mortification spreading quickly through my veins. I find myself dropping my chin and covering my face with my hand, all but dropping below the table to hide.

"What's happening?" he asks, worry marring his features. "Is everything okay?"

I peek through my fingers and sigh. "Yeah, everything's fine," I grumble, setting my phone down without replying. "Apparently, someone in the bar has been super busy since we arrived."

It only takes a second for realization to set in. He glances around, as if trying to read who might have already activated the gossip texting tree that flourishes in Mason Creek. I mean we're talking gold-star gossip here. Someone was probably already alerting their friends the moment we stepped through the doors together. "Wow, that didn't take long."

I sigh, throwing my napkin onto my plate and pushing it away. "I should have known. It's one of the main reasons I didn't miss small-town living."

He chuckles at my discomfort. "You get used to it."

"Hey, Malcolm," a woman practically sings as she walks by, running her finger across the back of his neck and sipping a fruity mixed drink.

"Did you?"

Malcolm seems to consider my question before he replies, "I guess. I'm just used to it. And I always seem to be a hot topic, which is probably why everyone has taken an interest in you tonight. I apologize if I put you in an uncomfortable position."

I take a quick look around the room, realizing that many patrons are looking our way. "It must be difficult, being the subject of town chatter all the time." I throw him a quick grin and wink, just to let him know I'm teasing.

He laughs once more, the sound causing my thighs to clench. "I suppose I keep the busybodies very occupied."

Understatement of the year, but I don't know him well enough to comment further, so I keep retorts to myself. "I should probably head home."

He nods, pulling out his wallet and dropping a handful of bills onto the table.

"I can pay for my meal," I offer, reaching into my wristlet for cash.

"I insist. I invited you to join me. Plus, I put you in the line of fire for town chatter." He waves off my hand, refusing to take my money.

Standing up, we make our way to the door. This time, Malcolm doesn't place his hand on my lower back, and I'm both glad and saddened by it. A part of me wants his touch and enjoyed it way too much the first time, but a bigger part doesn't want to add more fuel to the fire. I'm already going to have my hands full convincing my sister there's nothing between the mayor and me, but if we leave together touching, I'm sure it'll be front page blather in the *MC Scoop*, the local town gossip blog by Tate Michaels.

"Night," Malcolm hollers to Jack before opening the door for me. Outside, the night air is much cooler than the afternoon, causing me to shiver. As we approach the lot, he adds, "I appreciate you joining me for dinner."

"Thanks for the invite." I stop at my car and turn to face him. This is the point where I turn all awkward and uncomfortable. I've never been good talking to guys, which is probably why I don't date a lot. In fact, my serious boyfriends total a solid two, as does the number of guys I've slept with in the last decade.

God, I'm such a loser.

But I have a son to consider, and he comes first.

Always.

When he doesn't reply, I add, "I guess I'll see you around?"

Malcolm nods and opens my car door. "You will."

"Next Thursday," I blurt out, diving into the driver's seat.

"Next Thursday," he confirms, the slightest smile toying on his lips. Very full, very sexy lips. Delectable lips. Completely kissable lips.

Oh man, I have to stop thinking about them.

"Yes. Next Thursday." Now I sound like an idiotic parrot.

He grins widely, showing off his perfectly straight, white teeth. "Unless we run into each other before then." The way he says it lets me know I can probably expect to be running into him again. Malcolm tosses me a wink and shuts my door, tapping on the roof as I start the engine.

I pull from the lot and glance in my rearview mirror, finding Malcolm still standing there, watching me go. Something unsettling overcomes me.

I like that he's interested.

I like it a lot.

Chapter SEVEN

Malcolm

Is it weird I'm excited about the monthly finance committee meeting?

Yes, weird and completely out of character for me.

The finance committee is the one meeting I always dread, because there's always some argument about how the budgeted money should be used. But tonight, I'm excited to be here. Why? Because it's Monday, and Lenora cleans the building.

The moment we're done approving recommendations to take to the full city council next month, I adjourn the meeting and make my way to my office with minimal chitchat. Fortunately, there's a baseball game on tonight and half the council members are anxious to go home to watch the second half.

Before I step into my office, the sound of a vacuum in the front office catches my attention. I instantly smile. I've thought of her nonstop since Thursday night, which makes it very hard—pun intended—and uncomfortable during the workday. Nights weren't much better either. Except then, I could take care of that pesky problem in the privacy of my own bedroom. Or shower. Or office, like late last night.

I move to the large front office, where I find Lenora running the vacuum by Shana's desk. Her back is to me, which gives me the perfect view of her backside. She's wearing black leggings again, showing off her tanned calves and accentuating one of my favorite attributes.

Her ass.

Leaning against the wall, I watch her work. She's meticulous, as I discovered last Thursday night when she cleaned my house, going over the main traffic areas twice before moving on to another part of the office.

When she reaches the end of the room, she turns off the vacuum, spins around, and startles. "Jesus, Malcolm!" she bellows, covering her heart with her hands.

"Sorry," I reply with a chuckle. "I didn't mean to scare you."

"It's okay," she quickly insists, winding the cord for the vacuum around the handle, giving me another amazing view of her ass. "Is your meeting finished?"

"Just finished up."

"Okay. I'm almost finished here. That's my last room to clean," she says, wheeling the vacuum toward me to take it down the hall.

As she passes, I catch a whiff of something fruity, either lotion or shampoo, and all I want to do is find out where the scent is coming from by running my nose over every inch of her body.

"Have you already completed my office?" I ask, causing her to pause when she's beside me.

"I have. I started there."

A corner of my mouth tips upward. "Got that one done and out of the way while I was busy, huh?"

Leni blushes, those dangerous hazel eyes that appear in my dreams, gazing at me with embarrassment and wonder. "Yes, just to be safe."

I lean forward, invading her personal space, and have to refrain from kissing those perfect lips. "Too bad. I might have enjoyed the interruption again."

"Oh, Malcolm, you're still here."

Now it's my turn to startle and glance down the hallway toward the council chamber meeting room, but don't pull back from Lenora. "Raymond. I thought you were going home to catch the Dodgers game."

The older man's eyes sparkle with mischief as he grins at me, his eyes bouncing from Leni to me. "I was, but remembered we were going to discuss the meeting for the contract for the water treatment facility."

I almost chuckle, knowing there was no such discussion in the works. "Well, then we better step into my office. Shall we?" I ask, finally moving away from where Leni stands frozen in place. "Talk to you later, Lenora."

As much as I don't want to, I leave her standing in the hallway and join Raymond in my office. Even though I'd much rather stay with her, I need to put her and that delectable ass out of my mind and focus on my job. It is the reason I'm here, right? Not to stare at her.

Though, that doesn't sound like such a bad idea either.

Today was a bitch. I worked at the law firm all morning and had court at the county courthouse all afternoon. A case I thought was a slam dunk was anything but, and even though it ended in my client's favor, it was a long afternoon.

Now, all I want to do is go home and relax.

And spend the next few hours watching Lenora clean my house again.

It's Thursday evening, and I just pray I'll be there before she arrives. It's already almost seven, much later than I usually get home, but after court, I had to go back to the office for a while. Not only was my dad there, but my grandpa stopped by too, which resulted in me telling them about court and catching up on what's going on at a nearby golf course.

Now, I'm finally pulling into my driveway, happy to see I have arrived before Leni. I jump out, wishing I had time to shower, but knowing it's not going to happen. Unless I plan to have her find me standing in the bathroom naked again.

Not a bad idea, actually…

I park in the garage and hop out of my car. Before I can close the door, I hear a car pulling into the driveway. I set my briefcase down, prepared to offer to assist her with unloading her supplies, but can tell something's not right. Lenora gets out of her car looking frazzled. I'm heading in her direction immediately.

"What's wrong?" I ask, taking in the worry lines on her forehead and the way she pinches her lips together.

"Hey, listen, I think I need to reschedule," she replies in a hurry. "My dad fell and, it's probably just a sprain or something, but my mom had to take him to the hospital to get it checked out. I ran and picked up Trace as soon as I was finished at the physician's office. I called Laken, but they went shopping and won't be back to Mason Creek for another forty-five minutes or so, so it's probably best I come back another time. Maybe we can—"

"Breathe, Lenora," I whisper, wrapping my hands around her upper arms and giving them a comforting, gentle squeeze. "It's okay. We don't need to reschedule."

She takes a few deep breaths and meets my gaze. "I can come tomorrow night. I'm sure Laken will be able to help with Trace."

I'm already shaking my head. "No need. He's welcome here. I do believe I mentioned that last week."

She seems so unsure, narrowing her eyes as if she doesn't understand. "Yeah, but I just thought that was you being polite. The last thing either of us need is a five-year-old underfoot when I'm working."

"So I'll take him out back. He can play in the backyard."

I can't tell what she's thinking, and frankly, that bothers me. I've consistently been able to read women, but with Leni, she's always a mystery. A surprise I can't wait to unravel. "He probably won't want to leave my side. He doesn't know you."

I shrug. "That's fine too. I'm sure we can keep him busy in a place he can see you."

"But…"

"No buts, Leni. I don't mind Trace being here. I promise."

She stares at me for several seconds, those wheels turning in that big, beautiful brain of hers. After what feels like the longest five seconds ever, she nods. "Okay. As long as Trace is comfortable."

"Agreed." She turns to get Trace from the back seat when she stops and turns my way. "You called me Leni."

Shrugging, I reply, "It just seemed like you needed the security of your nickname in the moment."

She gives me an appreciative smile, one very different than I'm used to receiving from a woman. This one lacks the I-want-to-suck-your dick eyelash batting and is replaced by open and sincere gratitude.

I think I like this look a hell of a lot more.

Leni opens the back door and helps her son unfasten his seat belt. He hops out and gazes up—way up—and meets my eye. "Hi, Trace. I'm Malcolm."

The little boy directly stares at me, while moving to hide a bit behind his mom.

"Trace, this is Mr. Wright. I'm going to clean his house, okay? You can come inside with me, and if you're good and quiet while I work, we'll stop and get ice cream tomorrow from Twisted Sisters after dinner, okay?"

The little boy's hazel eyes widen with delight as he nods insistently. "Okay. I'll be good."

"I know you will be," she replies, ruffling the mop of dark brown hair on top of his head. "Do you want to help me carry my stuff?"

The little boy nods and grins the biggest toothless smile. I can't help but grin myself. I watch as they move to the trunk. Lenora takes out the plastic tote on wheels, and when she pulls the shoulder bag out, she hands it to Trace, who stumbles under the weight. I reach forward and steady the child, lifting the bag a little to help him carry his load. Together, we walk into the garage and through the mudroom door.

"Take off your shoes, Trace," Lenora says as she trails behind us into my house.

The boy kicks off his Velcro Batman sneakers and walks with me into the kitchen. "I'll take this," I state, lifting the bag off his shoulders and setting it on the counter.

I watch as Trace takes in my house, his curious eyes looking at my space from top to bottom. When they settle on the big bay window, he hesitantly moves in that direction, gazing out over the backyard and lake with a hint of a smile on his lips.

"Why don't you take a seat at the table," she instructs, pulling a notepad and pen from her bag, placing it in front of him. "I'll start in here."

While Lenora gets to work in the kitchen, I make my way to the refrigerator and grab a bottle of water. I'm not sure what kids drink, but I only have a couple of options to offer. Before I say anything, I check the expiration date on the half-gallon of milk, grateful when I see it still has a few days to go before it's no good.

"Hey, Trace. Would you like something to drink? I have water or milk," I offer, holding up a bottle of water and the carton of milk.

He glances up and turns to his mom. She gives him a smile and says, "You can pick."

He looks back my way, studying both for several long seconds before he points to the milk. "Please." His voice is quiet, yet polite, in a shy way that reminds me of his mom. Suddenly, I'm determined to pull a few grins and words from the little guy.

When I set the glass on the table, I notice he's drawing on the notepad Lenora gave him. The sketch is very child-like but clearly depicts a fish. As he sips on his milk, Trace keeps glancing to the side, his attention on the lake out back.

After a few minutes of him looking outside, an idea creeps in my mind. "Hey, Trace?" When he looks my way, I ask, "Would you like to go outside with me to see the lake?"

Excitement flashes in his eyes before he turns around in the chair to where his mom is working. Lenora stops, clearly hearing my question, her eyes bouncing between Trace and me.

"If it's okay with you, of course," I add rapidly.

"Oh, I'm not sure Trace will want to go," she replies hesitantly.

"I do!" he claims eagerly, his whole body vibrating with an enthusiastic energy.

"He's only had one week of swimming lessons." I can tell Leni's super nervous at the thought of him going outside without her.

I step forward until I'm standing directly in front of her. "I won't let him out of my sight, Leni. Promise. We'll go stand at the dock for a bit. The lake is low right now, and the water looks calm. It's safe."

She swallows hard and nods, squatting in front of Trace. "You be very careful, okay? You don't have a life jacket like when you went fishing with Papa, so you can't get too close to the edge of the dock. Listen to Mr. Wright."

"Okay, Mommy, I'll be good!" Trace assures, jumping up and running to get his shoes. "Ready!" he proclaims as soon as he slides his shoes on his feet.

I glance down and laugh. "You've got them on the wrong foot, Champ."

Trace looks down and shrugs before plopping on his rear and switching his shoes to the right foot.

"Holler if you need anything," Lenora says, her hazel eyes laden with anxiety. I don't necessarily feel she's anxious about me watching her son as she is about leaving him with someone she doesn't know well, nor does the boy. As a single mom living out of state, I imagine her circle was pretty small where Trace came from, especially if the father was in and out of their lives when it suited him.

"I will, promise. We'll be right outside."

With that, I slide open the back door, and Trace and I step under the warm sunshine. We slowly walk toward the water's edge, Trace never getting more than a foot or two away from me, but I can tell he's ready to go.

And in a way, I am too.

"Come on, Trace, let's go," I insist, taking off at a slow run.

The five-year-old follows suit, running after me with a giggle. I slow my pace and let him catch and pass me at the last second. "I'm the beater!" he professes as we reach the dock.

I huff out a deep breath dramatically. "You're a fast runner. You definitely beat me."

He smiles up at me, one of those big toothless grins, and suddenly, my heart lunges into my throat. It's so weird to me, this reaction. I'm rarely around kids. Have only been near one baby, and there was no way I was holding it. I've never felt this sense of pride and elation by one simple smile. But seeing this look on Trace's face just does something to me.

It makes me crave things I've never wanted before.

"Can we go out there?" he asks, pointing down the short dock.

"We sure can, but you have to stay right with me, all right?"

He nods solemnly and slips his hand inside my own. There's so much trust in those hazel eyes, it steals my breath and causes my heart to dance. I guide him down the dock, which is plenty big for two people to comfortably walk side by side. In fact, I've never been more grateful for the wide wooden structure that came with the house than I am right now.

We reach the end and just stare out at the water. Even though we're standing still, Trace doesn't remove his hand from my grasp, and I realize I'm content. Just me and this boy, watching the waves slowly roll our way.

Not the way I thought I'd spend my Thursday night, with a young boy standing beside me as I stare out over the serene waters of Baylor Lake, but I can't think of a better way to spend it.

Peaceful has taken on a whole new meaning.

Chapter EIGHT

Leni

I've been watching them out the window for the last five minutes. They're just standing at the end of the dock, watching the water and holding hands. I can see Trace pointing at a fish jumping, his attention quickly focused upward as Malcolm explains something to him. The sight causes a funny palpitation in my chest. One that's both reassuring and unsettling.

Trace's dad has been an unstable figure in his life. Since I met Greg, he's worked for the railroad, traveling all over the northern West Coast to build and help maintain rail systems. He would be gone for two-to-four-week stints, only to come home and go out all weekend, needing to unwind with his friends.

For the last half of our relationship, he had another house about two hours closer to the rail yard where he worked.

He said it was just easier that way.

Only, when he stayed there, he never seemed to find the time to come back to where we were. We weren't just second fiddle, we were third, somewhere behind his job and his friends. An inconvenience that was always waiting whenever he felt obligated to do his duty as a father.

That's why I had to move back home.

I didn't want Trace to ever feel like an inconvenience, and I knew, the older he got, the more he'd see. The worse he'd feel.

And I was tired of waiting. Of never knowing when he was going to come home, and in some cases, what shape he'd be in when he got there. If alcohol was more important than spending time with your family, then what's the point?

I had a family who was dying to spend more time with Trace, to get to know him better than just a few long weekends a year over holidays or summer break. When I made the decision to move, it felt like the right thing to do. I knew in my heart bringing Trace home to Mason Creek was what he needed.

What we both needed.

I packed everything up, rented the biggest U-Haul van I could get with my license, and drove myself home. The only person I told I was coming was my mom, which, in turn, meant my dad. They were both waiting at the edge of the sidewalk for me when I pulled that big monstrosity into their driveway. The whole thing, start to finish, took just over two weeks. I hated not telling Laken I was coming, but I just needed to get it done. Move. Be home. The explanations of why could come later.

I've been home almost six months now, and Greg hasn't reached out to me once.

Not. Once.

He has to know I moved, right? I mean, even after a few months, he'd at least pop in to see his son before darting off to some other part of the state again. Yet, I haven't heard one peep from him.

Maybe that's my fault. I suppose I should have reached out to him when I made the decision to relocate, but why? So I could tell his voicemail when he didn't answer? And why do I always have to carry this one-sided relationship? Haven't I earned a little more than a few random text messages and the occasional romp in the sheets when he's home?

The answer is yes.

That's why I didn't tell him.

I expected him to care enough to call. To care enough about seeing Trace to find out why we weren't in the small two-bedroom house anymore. I'd lived there since I was twenty-two and freshly out of college. God, he lived there with me for years, for crying out loud. Until he got his own place, essentially cutting us out of his life.

I tried to keep in touch. Even after we broke up—multiple times. I always texted him photos of Trace or funny stories about things he'd done. Every once in a while, he'd show up on my doorstep, declare he was going to be the dad and boyfriend we deserved. And then Monday morning would roll around, and he'd be gone again. Sometimes he'd keep in touch throughout the week, and other times, I could have been dying and I wouldn't have gotten a damn reply to save my life.

After a while, you just get tired of trying.

Now, as I glance out at my son and the man holding his hand, I'm struck with a sense of longing. Even though I'm not in any hurry to fill that father-figure void in Trace's life, the aching for it when I see them together is real. I try not to think too much into the picture they create, but it's hard. It's too...nice. Like a magazine cover or photo you'd print and hang over the fireplace.

But that's not in the cards.

At least not now.

I'm not here to find a father for my son. I'm here to be closer to my family and provide a stable home for him to grow up in. A lot of moms are both mother and father, and I'll do it too. Plus, Trace has my dad, who is one of the best father figures I know. Even though he was tough on Laken and me, he did it because he loved us, teaching us so many valuable lessons in life without us even realizing it.

Now, as an adult, it's how he and my mom raised us that I use as a model to raise my own son.

I force myself to look away, even though the mother inside of me is screaming to watch Trace. I still have a job to do, and I'm not getting much of it done by gazing out the window every two seconds.

I quickly finish the kitchen and dining room before moving to the living room and foyer. After I dust and vacuum, I straighten up a few books he has lying on the coffee table. They're World War II and Korean War biographies, which surprises me a little.

They're not exactly the light reading I'd expect an attorney and small-town mayor to enjoy.

Catching movement out of the corner of my eye, I glance out the large bay window in the kitchen to find Trace and Malcolm running to the edge of the property. I move with them, making sure to keep an eye on where they're headed. Malcolm unlocks the outbuilding and pulls open the door. A few seconds later, he emerges with two fishing poles and a tackle box, and Trace throws his hands in the air in victory.

They chat away, approaching the sliding back door. My eyes meet Malcolm's steady, reassuring gaze, and my heart can't help but skip a beat. "Hey," he says, sliding open the door. "Do you mind if we wet a line? We're going to stay on the bank though, not fish from the dock, since Champ doesn't have a life jacket."

Champ.

He calls my son Champ.

Talk about butterflies fluttering in my chest.

"No, I think that's fine. As long as you keep an eye on him," I remind, even though I don't need to.

"I got him, Lenora." Malcolm winks at me before stepping inside to grab something from the freezer. It's a bag of shrimp. "All right, Champ, this'll have to do for tonight. Maybe next time, I'll have something better to use," he adds, heading back outside with their bait.

"Yay! Big fat worms! Papa says those catch the big fat fish!"

"They do! And I'll have a life jacket for you next time so we can fish from the dock. I'll teach you to cast real far," he says as they head back out to the water. Trace turns around, smiling so widely I can see all of his missing teeth, and waves.

My heart.

By the time nine rolls around, I'm exhausted and ready to go home. Thursdays are a long day for me, since I work in the mornings at the laundromat selling my cleaning supplies from nine to eleven. A twelve-hour day really does a toll on this single mom.

When all of my supplies are packed up, I head for the back door to find my son. Since the sun has set, I'd like to think they're finished with their fishing excursion, but maybe not. It's way past Trace's bedtime, so I'm hoping getting him gathered up and in the car isn't a big production.

Opening the door, I'm pleasantly surprised to find them sitting on the back patio. They're each sitting in a chair, Trace's wide eyes glued to the man beside him as he listens to the story Malcolm's sharing. "So there we were, reeling in this huge bluefin tuna, and it took about two hours to get it in by hand, me and my buddy switching off every twenty minutes. I was exhausted, but there was no way we were letting that fish get away."

"How much did it weigh?" my son asks, leaning forward to not miss a detail.

"Five hundred pounds."

"Wow! That's huge!" Trace replies, his mouth dropping open.

"I've got a picture of us with the fish in my office. Next time you come back, I'll show you before we go fishing." Malcolm must sense my presence and glances over his shoulder and meets my gaze. "Hey."

"All done," I state unnecessarily.

He nods and stands. Trace follows suit.

"Mommy, guess what? We went fishing with shrimps and we caughted one. It was a catfish, like I caughted with Papa. And next week, Malc says I can come back and fish again. He'll show me the biggest fish he caughted."

I smile. "Hey, why don't you go inside and wait for me by my totes, okay?"

"Okay," he hollers right before running around me and into the house.

Malcolm stands directly in front of me, towering over me like a tree. I've always felt small, the shortest of my friends growing up. Heck, even my younger sister, Laken, is taller than me. But standing in front of Malcolm, I feel tiny. He's nearly a foot taller than my five-foot three-inch frame. "Sorry if I overstepped, but I've enjoyed hanging out with him and fishing," he says nervously, shoving his hands in his pockets.

"What did you mean by next week?"

"Well, while we were throwing that catfish back, it hit me. I have the equipment here, minus a small enough life jacket, which I can get. You can bring him with next Thursday when you clean, and we can hang out. I'll get some worms too."

I'm pretty sure my mouth is hanging open, but I don't really know what to say. He actually wants me to bring my son back? For two hours? Is he nuts? "I'm not sure," I start.

"It's ultimately your decision, Leni, but I just thought it'd be something fun for Trace to do. Plus, I really enjoyed hanging out with him," he says with a sheepish grin.

I want to argue. It's not his responsibility to watch my son while I work. He's the client, not the babysitter. And frankly, I don't really know him. Not well. Not on a personal level. Sure, I know how my heart seems to skip a beat when he fixes those warm chocolate eyes on me, and how my panties are practically useless when he smiles.

"Listen, Malcolm, I appreciate your assistance where Trace is concerned, but he's not your responsibility to watch."

"I know. He's yours, and I can tell just by spending these last two hours with him, you're doing a great job with him. He's a good kid."

I can't help but smile at the compliment. When you're parenting solo, you're constantly questioning every little decision you make and just trying not to mess up too much. It's exhausting, to be honest. "Thank you."

"Like I said, it's your choice, Leni. Just know he's welcome here. I'd love to take him fishing." He doesn't say anymore, just lets me know the decision is mine.

I nod in appreciation, grateful he's not pushing me to say yes. Turning to head inside to gather my belongings, something catches my attention. "What's that?" I ask, pointing to the pergola I didn't notice before. It has lattice around three sides for privacy, the side facing the back of the house completely open.

Malcolm glances over his shoulder before answering. "That's the hot tub."

Images parade through my mind. Dirty ones with a chiseled chest and water dripping down the hard, muscular planes. The same ones that have been keeping me company for the last week and a half.

He leans closer, his warm breath tickling my ear as he whispers, "Maybe some night I'll give you a private tour. Swimsuits optional."

I can't help but bark out a laugh. There he is. The cocky playboy I've come to expect. What's surprising is I seem to enjoy the playful banter more than I ever thought I would, which is probably why I reply with a shrug and say, "I've already seen the goods, but I suppose if you wanted to relax without your swimsuit, who am I to stop you?"

He chuckles and glances into the house. I turn and find Trace standing at the door, yawning. "I should get him home. It's way past his bedtime."

"It is. I'll walk you to your car," he replies, pulling open the sliding glass door and waiting for me to enter first. "Ready to go, Champ? Want to help me carry your mom's things to the car?"

Trace jumps right in, grabs for the tote. Of course, he needs assistance, since it's heavier and awkward.

I don't even have an opportunity to retrieve my own things. The boys grab it all and head for the front door, careful not to upend the plastic tote on wheels. Outside, they load my trunk, and all I can do is stand back and watch. Their interaction is so easy, natural. If Malcolm was ever nervous around my son, he's not showing it now. In fact, he looks very comfortable, which is a pleasant surprise.

Malcolm grabs the back driver's side door and pulls it open. "All right, Champ. Time to go home and get some sleep."

"But I was good, right? I get ice cream?" he asks, his tired, hopeful eyes eager for an answer.

Malcolm looks over at me for confirmation, to which I give a slight nod. "You sure were, Champ. So good, I think you should get two scoops. No, make it three."

I sigh and shake my head. Of course, there's a small smile on my lips too. "You're trouble, Mr. Mayor."

He waggles his eyebrows and gives me that smug grin. "Don't I know it." Once Trace is secured into his seat, he shuts the door and opens mine.

"Thank you." I don't just mean him opening my door, and I can tell he understands by the way he smiles.

"You're welcome."

I slip into my seat and reach for the handle. "We'll see you next week."

His eyes light up. "Does that mean you'll bring him with you?"

"Yes." I realize instantly I want to. Their interaction, albeit somewhat brief, did this mom's heart good. Trace looked comfortable and got to enjoy some time doing an activity he's growing to love.

"Can't wait," he replies with a big smile.

He shuts my door and waves at Trace, stepping back and out of the way while I pull from his driveway. Malcolm remains standing there until I turn the corner and am out of sight, solidifying this growing attraction I feel toward him. It's not just how he is with me—flirty, yet attentive—but now that I've seen this different side of him, the one directed at my son, I feel this whole new wave of fascination.

And damn it, even though I should be more cautious since Trace is involved, I want to see where it goes.

I just pray it doesn't bite me in the ass.

Chapter NINE

Malcolm

I grab my phone and send the message I've been contemplating for the last fifteen minutes.

Me: How's the ice cream?

I know she's there. I have an unobstructed view of the ice cream stand across the park from my office window. Ever since I arrived at City Hall, I've been watching for them, wondering what time she'd bring him over for his reward. I can't tell if Trace got the triple scoop, like I suggested, but I can tell he's having fun. I can see his smile all the way over here.

My phone chimes with a message, and I can't believe how anxious I am to see it. I've never been this guy. The one who waits with bated breath for the woman to respond. Yet here I am, palming my phone so I don't risk missing it.

Lenora: Excellent.

And then a photo pops up. One of Trace, smiling a big toothless grin at the camera, ice cream and chocolate syrup smeared all over his lips.

My heart somersaults in my chest as I grin at the image and save it to my phone.

Me: Is that a triple scoop of swirl ice cream?

Lenora: It is. With chocolate syrup and sprinkles.

Me: Wow, he must have been really, REALLY good!

Lenora: Or someone told him he deserved three scoops, so he wasn't letting me get away with not buying him three scoops. *insert devil grinning emoji*

Me: *insert angel emoji*

Me: He deserves it. I'll even buy since it was my mouth that got you into that situation.

Lenora: Not necessary.

Wanting to keep the conversation continuing, I ask:

Me: So what kind did you get? Triple scoop of rocky road? Cookie dough? Key lime pie?

Lenora: Just a single scoop of plain vanilla for me.

Me: What in the ice cream blasphemy is that?!?! *insert shocked emoji*

Lenora: I'm trying to watch what I eat, but since I'm not strong enough to resist ice cream, I kept it simple.

I groan. A diet? Fuck no. Lenora is damn gorgeous. Sure I'm attracted to her beautiful smile and her alluring eyes, but also the rest of her. Her body is sexy as hell, the things wet dreams are made of. No way does she need to lose weight, and it kinda pisses me off that she thinks she does.

Me: No. Go get some chocolate syrup on that thing. Sprinkles and whipped cream too. You're beautiful just the way you are. You don't need to diet.

She doesn't reply right away, and I wonder if I overstepped, but dammit, she needs to hear it. She's simply stunning, especially with her large boobs and wider hips.

Finally, after a long minute, she replies.

Lenora: That's kind of you to say, but I do. Ever since I had Trace, my boobs and ass have developed their own zip codes.

Me: Fuck that. Your boobs and ass are perfect.

Lenora: Of course a man would say that. The bigger the boobs, the better, right?

Me: Nope. I don't say anything I don't mean, sweetheart.

Lenora: They're way too big for my short body. Everyone thinks so.

Me: False. And it sounds like you've been hanging around some real jerks.

Lenora: You may have a point there, Wright.

Lenora: I can't believe I'm talking about this with you. Am I making you uncomfortable?

Me: Just in the pants area, Lenora. They're suddenly...tight.

I continue watching them out the window, wondering if I went too far. She needs to know her body is perfect, despite what she feels are imperfections. I've known a lot of women who are rail-thin and still pour on the "I'm fat" bullshit, but it's just to get compliments. In the short amount of time I've known Leni, I already know that's not what she's doing. She's speaking her mind, her truth. She's not fishing for accolades. She's telling me like it is, how she sees herself.

Well, fuck that.

It's time she knew how I see her.

Grabbing my phone and wallet, I shut down my computer and turn off the light. I push through the back door, making sure it's secure behind me and walk through the park, heading for the ice cream stand.

Trace spots me first, since he's facing my direction, and waves frantically.

"Hey, Champ. Mind if I join you for ice cream?" I ask, stopping at the place where they sit only long enough to see him nod. It kills me to not look at her, but I keep my focus on the boy. She's wearing shorts, her long, tanned legs on full display, and a low-cut V-neck T-shirt. Her long hair is down and blowing in the warm breeze. I know if I glance her way, I'm liable to pop a boner right here in the middle of the town park on a Friday night.

Families. Children. Ice cream. It would be all over the gossip chats before I could even finish my double scoop.

"Okay, I'll be right back."

I jump in line to order and make small talk with a few of the locals. The young couple directly in front of me just got married a few weeks ago, so I make sure to congratulate them on their nuptials. By the time they finish telling me about their honeymoon in Aruba, it's their turn to order. I wait patiently, making sure not to glance back at Trace and Lenora so I don't seem too anxious.

Finally, it's my turn to order. Of course, the moment I step forward, I see both Hattie and Hazel Jackson behind the counter, bickering about something.

"I'm telling you, we've sold more chocolate than vanilla," Hattie proclaims, her bluish hair even brighter under the lighting.

"I wasn't arguing about that, Hattie," Hazel retorts, her bright red hair and lips matching the maraschino cherries they serve on the sundaes.

I can't help but smile as they continue to bicker about ice cream flavors. Hattie is in a typical plaid shirt with blue jeans, while her sister is wearing a white ruffled top and blue slacks. Hazel definitely looks like she just got back from church.

"You were too, Hazel. I heard what you were mumbling under… Oh! Mayor Wright. We didn't see you there," Hattie states, stepping up to the counter and pulling an ink pen from behind her ear.

"Mayor Wright, please excuse my sister. She's out of sorts tonight. It's an honor to see you this evening. How are your parents?"

I give the older women a smile. "They're doing well, thank you for asking."

"Out of sorts," Hattie bellows in disbelief. "You're the one arguing about which flavor we sold more of tonight."

"Oh, hush, now! Malcolm, what can we get you tonight?" Hazel asks, taking the pen from her sister's hand and leaning over the counter.

"I'll take a double scoop of vanilla with banana split toppings, please."

"Coming right up!" Hattie bellows the second I place my order.

Hazel sighs and inputs the order into the register. I hand her a five-dollar bill to cover my ice cream and take the offered dish once Hattie has it ready. "Thanks, ladies. It was a pleasure seeing you."

"Oh, you too, Malcolm. Will we be seeing you run past our place later this evening? You know, it's the highlight of our day," Hazel says slyly with a big ol' grin on her face.

I bark out a laugh. "If that's the best excitement you ladies have, I think you need to get out more," I tease, throwing them a wink before waving goodbye. "Have a good evening."

"You too, Mayor!" they sing together.

Hattie glances around me and adds, "Oh, I think that's Lenora Abbott over there. Rumor has it you two had dinner at Pony Up last week."

Shaking my head, I turn and walk away, the sound of their laughter trailing behind me as I go.

I head to where Lenora and Trace sit. She's done with her plain vanilla by the time I sit beside her son, and he's busy stirring the chocolate syrup into the melted ice cream. "What kind did ya get?" he asks, eyeing my dish. "Are those bananas?"

"Yep. It's a banana split dish, so there's strawberries, pineapple, and chocolate syrup, along with banana chunks. Wanna try it?" I ask, pushing my dish his way.

Trace nods, licks his spoon, and shoves it into my ice cream, securing a big heap of the sweet treat.

"Trace!" Lenora chastises. "That's not nice. Mr. Wright was offering you a small bite, not half his sundae."

The boy gives me a sheepish grin before scraping part of the mixture off his spoon. I reach my own utensil into the dish and take a much smaller bite. "How is it?" I ask as he sucks the contents off his spoon.

"Dood!" he replies, his mouth full.

I can't help but chuckle as I push the bowl closer to Leni. "You're next."

"I'm not eating your ice cream."

I go ahead and scoop a variety of toppings with a little ice cream onto my spoon and hold it out. "Just try it. It's way better than the boring ol' vanilla you just had."

She holds her lips shut tightly, making me smile. "That's all I wanted."

Moving my spoon in her direction, I make the airplane noise, like I've seen in movies or TV commercials, resulting in Trace giggling. "You gots to, Mommy! The airplane is coming," he announces, making the sound right along with me.

I wave the spoon in front of her lips, touching the tip and leaving a trace of cream behind. My cock jumps with excitement, but I ignore it, trying to keep my focus away from all the dirty things that want to enter my mind.

Trace laughs, making Leni smile. She tries not to open her mouth as she does it, but as I drag more mess across her lips, she finally grins widely and giggles. That's when I shove the spoon between her lips and try not to groan as they cover the plastic. I do well until she releases the utensil and licks the tip of the spoon.

That's when a painful noise spills from my lips. It's deep and dirty, just like the parade of naughty thoughts flipping through my brain. Ones of her tongue licking...*things.*

Well, one specific thing.

And then I remember where I am and who I'm sitting next to, and guilt replaces those very vivid daydreams. It's a horrible cycle of being sexually aroused and then embarrassed because of where you're at, and the fact it keeps happening with Lenora is awfully telling. I can't stop thinking about her.

Wanting her.

I'm pretty sure I hear a camera click as I remove my spoon from her sexy-as-hell lips, but I ignore the implication. If someone *did* snap a picture of me, there's nothing I can do about it. Hopefully it was just a mom taking a quick photo of her kids eating their ice cream. With any luck, that'll be the image floating around social media, and not one of me feeding a woman ice cream, most likely with lust written all over my face.

But my luck isn't that good where potential gossip is concerned. I'm usually one of the first to get talked about somewhere, which is fine. I'm used to it. Hell, most of the time, it's because I've given the busybodies a reason to talk. Whatever. But the thought of them focusing on Lenora because of me doesn't sit right. I don't want her name tarnished because someone thought I was trying to seduce her with ice cream in the middle of the park, with her son right there. She's trying to run a business, and well, she deserves better.

"Thank you," she mumbles, grabbing a napkin and wiping off her lips. Even though I'd much rather she use her tongue, I'm kind of glad she didn't. I'd likely die from blood loss, with all of it flowing to one concentrated area, and that's not how I want to be remembered.

"You're welcome," I reply, scooping up a bite of the cold treat and eating it, liking the thought of my mouth touching something hers just touched.

I listen to Trace retell the story of catching our fish last evening, and I'm surprised I'm still as invested in it today as I was yesterday. I can picture his eyes as we reeled in that fish, even though it wasn't a very big one. He watched with curiosity as I carefully removed the hook and explained why we were going to throw it back. "So it can keep growing bigger and bigger," he tells his mom, finishing the story.

She just smiles, the side of her head resting against her palm. When her gaze turns to mine, she says, "It was all he talked about last night at bedtime."

"We didn't read a book from Aunt Laken's store because it was late. But tonight, I gets to pick out two books to read."

"Two books, huh?" I ask, moving my ice cream toward him as I see him eyeing what's left in my dish.

"Two!" he declares right before shoving his spoon back into my treat and taking a big bite.

I let him finish it off before collecting all of the trash from our small table. As I walk toward the nearest receptacle, I hear a familiar voice. "There you are. I haven't seen you in weeks. I thought maybe you were avoiding me."

Jessa.

What in the hell is she doing here, in the park, at the ice cream stand? This is definitely not her hangout.

I turn around and meet her gaze, surprisingly unhappy to see her. Not because she's a bad person or anything, but because she's a reminder of the man I am. The one who dates a lot of women because he has no intention of ever settling down with one. That's the guy I've always been, yet for some reason, he seems like someone I don't really know.

Or like.

"Hey, Jessa. What are you doing here?" I ask, shoving my hands into my pockets and rocking back on my heels.

She smiles, her lips painted a coral pink color. "Aren't you happy to see me?" she asks, batting her eyelashes as she steps forward and tips her cheek toward me.

I know what she wants, but I'm not really interested in giving it to her. However, not wanting to make a scene, my intention is to place a chaste, quick kiss on her cheek, making sure my hands remain in my pockets.

Just as my lips are about to connect with her cheek, she turns, our lips meeting. I go completely still, shocked that this is happening.

Right here.

Right now.

"Malcolm!"

I rip my mouth from hers and turn, my eyes slamming into Trace's.

And then his mother's.

Shit.

This doesn't look good.

Chapter TEN

Leni

Okay, so this isn't what I expected.

Malcolm turns, his wide, startled eyes locking on mine. He was just kissing this woman. No, not just any woman.

Jessa Donaldson.

Everyone knows Jessa. She's a stunningly beautiful woman with money. Her estate is one of the largest in the area, a whopping three thousand square foot home with five bedrooms and five bathrooms. Yes, five. What would a single woman need with five bathrooms?

I know this because I clean her home every Monday morning.

Tonight, she's well put together, wearing linen pants and a silk top that probably cost more than what I made all week. Her hair is expensive salon quality styled and her makeup flawless, but what really pulls my attention is the possessive hand she lays on Malcolm's arm.

"Hey, Champ," Malcolm replies, glancing back down at my son with a tight smile.

"We just came to say goodbye. It was nice seeing you again," I state as I reach down and take Trace's hand in my own. "Have a good evening," I add politely, offering a small grin to the woman standing across from me, watching me with hawk-like, laser-focused, green eyes.

The grin on her pink lips is calculating, and truthfully, it makes me uncomfortable. "I'll see you Monday, right?"

I nod. "I'll be there."

"I can walk you—" Malcolm starts, but I stop him with the shake of my head.

"Not necessary," I interrupt. "We walked here. Enjoy your evening." Glancing down at Trace, who's gaze is fixed on Malcolm. "Ready?"

He nods. "Bye, Malcolm. See you later!"

Malcolm gives Trace a friendly smile. "Bye, Champ. I'll see you soon."

Trace waves over his shoulder as we walk away. I can feel eyes on me. Not just Malcolm's, and probably Jessa's, but those of everyone around us. I keep my head up, don't meet their gaze, and head straight through the park in the direction of home. I swear I can hear their whispers trailing behind me.

That's the one big thing I didn't miss while I was away from this small town.

"It's bath time," I announce, cutting through the park and heading for the sidewalk.

"Do I gots to?" Trace whines, pulling a face.

"Yes, you have to. You're wearing as much ice cream as you ate tonight. If you don't take a bath, then you'll get bugs in your bed."

"Cool," Trace replies with humor dancing in his eyes.

"Not cool, little man. You know the rule: no bugs in the house."

His energy carries us through the park and down the sidewalk as he tells me all about bugs. We approach the back door of the laundromat and I pull the key from my pocket. One thing I've appreciated about the setup of the business is that the upstairs apartment still has a completely separate back entrance from the laundry services in the front. Plus, the stairs are on the inside, which means I don't have to deal with trying to get groceries up icy stairs in the winter or the metal railing scorching Trace's hands under the summer sun.

While he's in the tub, I finally let myself stop and replay everything that happened tonight. Malcolm was the one who texted me first. He's the one who showed up in the park while we were eating ice cream. I guess that's why I'm confused. Why show up and sit with us, spending time and sharing dessert, if he was going to cast us aside so quickly?

Looking up and seeing him kiss Jessa was like someone dumped a bucket of ice water over my head in the middle of January. It was unexpected, that's for sure.

But was it really?

Malcolm's reputation for being a playboy precedes him. From what I've been told since my return to town, he's dated everyone who's single in Mason Creek, the county, and probably half the state of Montana. He likes women and doesn't hide the fact. So why am I so surprised to see him kiss someone tonight? Maybe because it happened five seconds after he got up from my table? He didn't even make it ten feet away before he was locking lips with another woman.

That's fine.

That's his prerogative.

It's not like we're dating or anything.

Quite the opposite, actually.

All tonight did was reiterate the fact I don't want or need a relationship—with Malcolm or anyone else. Men aren't worth the hassle.

If only I really believed that.

My phone vibrates on my nightstand, interrupting my attempt at falling asleep. I crack open my eyes and glance at the alarm clock. Twelve thirty. Panic sets in that something's wrong with my parents or my sister, so when I grab my phone and tap on the screen, I'm surprised when I see Malcolm's name.

Before I can even pull up the text app, more texts come in a rapid-fire sequence.

Malcolm: I know it's late, and I'm sorry for that.

Malcolm: I can't sleep.

Malcolm: I keep replaying what happened earlier and I don't like it.

Malcolm: I've been telling myself this can wait until later, but the fact is, it can't.

Malcolm: I have something to say, and I'm afraid if I don't say it now, I'll chicken out.

Malcolm: First off, I'm sorry for how it probably looked earlier at the park. I wasn't expecting Jessa to be there, not that I know her schedule. We're friends, despite how that kiss looked. Hell, we're not even really friends.

Malcolm: To be completely blunt, we've been fuck buddies off and on for a year. I haven't seen her in the last two months though. She reached out to me last week, but I wasn't interested in hooking up.

Malcolm: Why? There's this other woman I can't stop thinking about, and she invades my thoughts night and day. She's gorgeous and has the most beautiful smile. She also has a pretty great kid, and believe it or not, I like spending time with him. I never would have thought it'd be possible, but it's true.

Malcolm: Honestly, I really want to see where it could go with her, but I'm afraid I've fucked it up already. I didn't initiate the kiss. I didn't even respond to it. But I was so shocked, I didn't do what I should have and pulled away immediately.

Malcolm: What I did do was make you uncomfortable. I know because I was just as uncomfortable, and it was written all over your face. Sure, you tried to hide it behind a smile, but I saw it.

Malcolm: And didn't like it.

Malcolm: I tried to push my uneasiness aside, pretend it wasn't there. All night, I kept telling myself it was better for you if I stayed away. You deserve someone who can give you exactly what you need. Someone who doesn't have to have his hand held throughout the relationship because he has no fucking clue what he's doing.

Malcolm: But the truth is I don't want to walk away.

Malcolm: I want to be that person, even if you deserve better.

Malcolm: And that doesn't scare me as much as I thought it would. I mean it does. I'm terrified because I've never done anything more than casual dating. But the prospect of MORE has me all sorts of wired like I drank too much caffeine.

Malcolm: So there you go. My middle of the night confession.

Malcolm: I see you're up and reading these. I'm sorry if I woke you, but I couldn't wait another minute to tell you. Maybe I'm a chickenshit for sending it in a text, but I wanted to make sure I said everything I wanted to say.

Malcolm: And that is I'm sorry. I want to see you again and hang out. I want to take you on a date.

I know you're a single mom, so if we have to take Trace with us, that'd be OK too. He's a cool kid.

Malcolm: OK, I'm gonna stop now. I've never been one to word vomit, especially in text form, and I'm doing an exceptional job at it tonight. I hope to see you again soon, and until I do, I know who'll be on my mind.

Malcolm: You.

Malcolm: Good night. Sorry to wake you.

I read through the long series of texts, my heart hammering in my chest. When I get back down to the end, my fingers hover over the screen, waiting for the cue to type. It comes only a few seconds later, my desire to talk to him overruling any hesitation I may feel.

Me: You didn't wake me.

The bubbles appear almost instantaneously.

Malcolm: I'm glad.

Malcolm: I had a good time tonight. You know, before...

I can't help but smile. I had a great time too, before Jessa Donaldson walked up and slammed her lips against his. Suddenly, I had felt the exact same as I did when Greg would go out with his friends the moment he got home. I felt unimportant. Invisible. Used.

Me: I enjoyed you joining us for ice cream. It was a pleasant surprise.

Malcolm: Maybe we can do it again sometime.

Me: Maybe we can.

Malcolm: As much as I'd love to stay up all night, talking to you, I know you need your sleep. Something tells me Trace is a ball of energy.

Me: All day, every day. He gets up at 5:30. In the morning. Who gets up that early for no good reason?

Malcolm: *hides eyes* Guilty.

Of course he does. He probably gets up to work out or run. You don't get a body like the naked one I saw in his office bathroom by eating donuts for breakfast and binge watching *The Office* whenever you can. He's not all bulky muscle though. Malcolm is defined in the sexiest way possible. He's lean and just...hard.

So. Hard.

I wiggle a bit under my comforter, trying to relieve the sudden ache between my legs at the onslaught of memory, but it doesn't help. Nothing ever helps.

Malcolm: Good night, beautiful. I look forward to seeing you again soon.

Me: Night.

This time when I rest my head on the pillow, I feel myself relax. Closing my eyes, it only takes minutes before I feel sleep wrap around me, drawing me in. With a smile on my lips, I succumb to it with dreams of Malcolm Wright carrying me away.

Chapter ELEVEN

Malcolm

"Hey, Malcolm. How have you been?"

I turn around and find Grady Jackson standing behind me. He was a few years younger than me in school, but I know him well enough to consider him a friend. Hell, I guess everyone is your friend in this town, but I've always liked Grady. "Good, man. You?"

"Can't complain." He spots what I'm holding in my hand and gives me a quizzical look. "That's probably a little small for you," he teases, referring to the child's life jacket I'm holding.

I chuckle and give him a glance. "Yeah, it definitely wouldn't fit me." Then something hits me. "You have a small child. Would you say this fits a five-year-old?" I ask, holding it up. I went off the size chart on the cardboard tag attached and tried to guestimate Trace's height and weight.

He looks it over. "Yeah, that's the size I have for Jillian, and she's not quite five. That should work."

Nodding, I tuck the vest under my arm. "I appreciate the help." I wait for him to ask more, but Grady's never been one to dig for dirt like so many of the others in town.

"No problem," he says, turning to head a little farther down the aisle. "Did you hear Tucker's playing this Saturday at Pony Up? Charlee's really wanting to go up and hear him play. I think Grayson and Laken are going too, if you're interested."

I nod, appreciating the invitation. "Thanks, I'll definitely keep that in mind."

He holds up a hand to wave. "See ya around."

Grady disappears down an aisle while I take my purchase to the counter. Once I've paid and the new life jacket is in a bag, I walk back to the office just down the block, prepared to get a little work done before I need to go to City Hall. Of course, as soon as I walk in, my dad is sitting in the lobby, and he's talking to none other than my grandpa.

"Malcolm," my grandpa's boisterous voice booms through the seating area.

"Hey, Grandpa. What are you doing here?" I ask, noticing our secretary, Elaina, isn't here and probably out to lunch.

"I was on my way to grab some tortilla shells. Grandma has a taste for tacos for dinner, but we're out of shells, so I volunteered to run to the grocery store."

"Grandma has a hankering for tacos?" I can't help but chuckle. My grandparents are the best ever. Despite being wildly successful before retirement, they've always been down to earth and cool like that.

"Yep. You interested in joining us?" he offers, his eyes bouncing between my face and the bag in my hand.

"Sorry, I'm unavailable. I have plans," I tell him, setting my bag down, yet trying to keep the contents concealed by the chair.

"Plans? They wouldn't happen to be with a certain brunette who owns a local business and has a small son, would they?" the oldest Wright asks, his lips turned upward as he waits.

I look at my dad, who just holds up his hands. "Don't look at me. I didn't say anything."

"He didn't have to," Grandpa declares. "You know this town better than that, Malcolm. Your grandma's phone was chirping before you even left the park last Friday night."

I sigh, really disliking the chatter more now than ever before. "I'm sure she got an earful," I reply, taking a seat and crossing my arms over my chest.

He shrugs. "You know a lot of the stuff is hearsay anyway, but since you didn't deny it, I'll take at least part of the story as fact."

Dammit.

"I've hung out with Lenora Abbott a few times," I confirm but go into no more detail.

"And I take it the life jacket in that bag you're trying to hide behind the chair is for her son?"

I sigh and close my eyes, suddenly wishing I hadn't come back to the office so quickly. "Had I known I was going to encounter the Spanish Inquisition, I'd have gone for coffee first," I state, making both men laugh. "Yes, the vest is for Trace, Lenora's five-year-old son. I'm taking him fishing today, while Leni works. She had a family emergency last week and ended up bringing him with her, so we went out back while she cleaned. The boy's a fan of fishing, so I thought we'd go."

"Ahh, yes, I saw Lisa Abbott at the post office earlier in the week. Lewis took a bit of a tumble and sprained his ankle pretty good. I guess he's on crutches for a week or two," Grandpa says to my dad before turning his gaze back to me. When he does, he just smiles a wide, knowing grin.

"What?" I ask, hating that he can read me so damn well. He's always been able to tell what I'm thinking, from the time I was a young boy until now. It's one of the many qualities that made Grandpa an amazing lawyer.

My tone apparently amuses him, and he laughs. When he sobers, he just says, "You like her."

I scoff in denial, but it's useless. Instead of the confession he's anticipating, I say, "I barely know her."

Grandpa shrugs. "What does that matter? Every relationship has a beginning. I barely knew your grandma when I met her, even though we were both raised right here in Mason Creek. She was just young enough I knew of her but didn't know any of the things that mattered. Those things I learned along the way, but I decided to try because I was attracted to her, and I needed to know more."

I pull a face. "Please don't go into any more details about your attraction."

Grandpa lets a hearty laugh rip. "You don't want to hear how your father got here?"

"Dad, we've all heard the Chevy Bel Air story. Please spare us," my dad replies.

Grandpa holds up his hands in surrender. "Fine, fine. I won't talk about the night your mom and I went parking on our way to the Davis Bridge, the one the old man built for his wife on private property. All the kids used to sneak back there and kiss."

Dad snorts. "Sounds like they did more than park."

"Still do," I mumble aloud.

"My point is, you've got to take a risk to reap the reward, Malcolm."

"Thank you, Grandpa. This has been an educational and slightly nauseating conversation," I state, standing up and grabbing the bag. "If you'll excuse me, I have a few hours of work I need to finish."

As I turn to head to my office, Grandpa hollers, "Have fun tonight. I hear the fish are biting."

Waving, I secure myself inside my office, ready to get to work. The sooner I complete my to-do list, the quicker I'm home and fishing with my new little friend.

And out of all the things I could do tonight—all the women I could be with—the thought of it being anyone but them is unfathomable.

"Malcolm!" Trace hollers, running up the driveway to where I stand.

"Hey, Champ. Are you ready to go fishing?" I ask, dropping to my knees in front of him.

"Yep! I broughted my Spider-Man pole," he informs.

"Great. Let's help your mom get her stuff inside and settled, and then we'll go wet a line, okay?"

"Okay!" Trace runs back to the trunk of the car and helps Leni remove her things. The third and final item she pulls out is a short Spider-Man pole with bright green line and a red and white bobber.

"You carry the pole, and I'll help your mom with this tote," I inform the little guy, who carefully handles the fishing device, carrying it into the garage.

"It doesn't have a hook on it. My dad removed it after their excursion because Trace kept wanting to play with it," Lenora says, trailing behind as we step inside the mudroom.

"I'll take care of it," I tell her, holding the door open for her to enter. "Probably smart of him," I add, glancing back to see Trace pretending to cast beside my car.

"Trace, not too close to Mr. Wright's car, please," she hollers before stepping inside completely.

The little boy runs inside, excitement radiating from his tiny body, as he helps his mom unpack her things. The second he has the last item set on the floor, he turns to face her with big, hopeful eyes. "Can I go now?"

She grins at her son. "You have to listen to Malcolm the whole time, okay? And be very careful."

He sighs, as if he's heard her request for caution many times in the past. "I be careful, Mommy."

"And I bought a life jacket," I add, hoping to ease some of the worry lines around Leni's eyes.

She looks up, meeting my gaze, and gives me a grateful smile. It sends my heartbeat into stroke-level territory, and I don't know why. I've never reacted to a simple grin before, not the way I do with hers. "Thank you."

I'm pretty sure she's not just referring to the life jacket I purchased.

I nod and turn to Trace. "Ready to go, Champ?"

"Yes!" he bellows, throwing his hands in the air and running to grab his fishing pole.

"Do you need me for anything?" I ask, happy to see her for the first time since last Friday night at ice cream. Even though we've texted a few times randomly since, I haven't locked eyes on her in six long days. Monday night, my committee meeting went long, resulting in her already leaving the building by the time I was finished, which sucked because I really wanted to see her.

"I'm fine, thank you," she replies, those gorgeous hazel eyes a little brighter than usual.

Nodding, I state, "Holler if you need anything. We'll just be out back."

I watch her gather what she needs for the kitchen and begins her work. It's weird I could stand here and watch her work the entire time, but that's not going to happen. There's a little boy with his face practically pressed against the sliding door, anxiously waiting for me to join him outside.

I already dug out what we needed from the shed and placed it on the back patio. The new life jacket, worms, net, and a small tacklebox is ready to go. "All right, Trace, let's put on your life jacket and take our stuff to the dock."

He shows me his missing teeth as he grins up at me. "That's the same colors as my pole," he declares as I hold up the red and white striped vest.

"It is." I make sure it's secure and tight before picking up the box of supplies and container of worms.

"Where's yours?"

I stop and face the child. "My what?" He pulls on his life jacket. "Oh, I didn't bring one for me."

"Mommy says you should always have a life jacket around the water."

His words are simple, yet a direct reminder of how much his mother loves him. "Then I should probably put one on too, huh?"

Trace nods eagerly and follows me to the shed. Honestly, I don't know when the last time I wore one was. I don't wear it when I kayak or canoe, mostly because I'm a great swimmer. But they always say lead by example, right? That's why I dig one out of the shed, blow off the dust, and slip it on over my T-shirt.

Finally, we're all set to go fishing.

I find myself explaining everything to a very curious little boy as I secure the hook onto his line and bait it. He giggles as the worm wiggles against my fingers, leaving smears of dirt in its wake. When the pole is finally ready to cast, we take position at the end of the dock.

"You got this, Champ?" I ask, handing over the pole.

Trace nods eagerly, presses the big red button, draws back the pole, and lets it fly. Considering it's a small kid's pole, he does a great job.

"Perfect," I compliment, reminding him to set the line.

Then, we take a seat at the end of the dock. Our feet dangle, but mine are much closer to the water than his. He swings them anxiously but tries to keep his pole as still as possible. Every once in a while, he'll reel a bit of his line, making sure to keep it tight. Considering he's only five, he's doing very well with what his grandpa clearly taught him.

After only a few minutes, he gets a bite. "Very slowly get ready to set the hook," I whisper, watching as the bobber dips below the water. "Now."

Trace jerks back on the pole, setting the hook inside the fish's mouth, and starts to reel. The end of the small pole bends downward, but if he's struggling to pull it in, he doesn't show it.

"Nice and steady, Champ. You got it," I state, standing up and grabbing the net. When he gets the fish to the surface, I drop to my knees and scoop it up. Trace jumps up now, kneeling right beside me and watching in utter fascination as I bring his catch onto the dock. "Look at the size of that catfish."

"It's huge!" he declares, o

bviously proud of his fifteen-inch catfish.

"It sure is. Stand up and you can hold your fish. I'll take a picture for your mom."

He does, lifting his pole and grabbing the line. I help him get into position and grab my phone. I'm able to snap a handful of pictures with Trace grinning proudly as he holds up his big catch. He struggles to keep holding up the fish, so I step in and grab the line.

With the fish back on the dock, he bends over, watching my every move as I grab pliers from the tacklebox and carefully remove the hook. When it's free of the sharp object, I lift the fish carefully, and hold it up. "Do you want to hold it?"

He observes the fish for a few seconds before nodding.

"You have to do it like this," I show him, "or the fins might poke you." I take his little hands and replace mine with his.

He instantly starts to giggle. "It's slippery!"

"It is," I agree, grabbing my phone once more and taking a picture of him checking out his fish and not even caring that I'm getting the device dirty.

I explain where the catfish can get you, the fins puncturing your skin and causing discomfort and pain. Trace listens intently, soaking up everything I say like a little sponge. I place the fish on a stringer line and slowly lower it back into the water, securing the lock on the post of the dock. Then, I grab the pliers and make sure the hook is ready to go.

"Are we done now?" he asks, disappointment evident in his question.

I smile and squeeze his shoulder. "No, Champ. We're just getting started."

Chapter TWELVE

Leni

"Call me if you have any problems," I tell my mom but don't meet her gaze. I already know she's shaking her head at my statement.

"We'll be fine, Leni. He's been talking about this sleepover with Harlow and Hayden for days. He can't wait to tell them all about the fish he caught Thursday evening," she says, not even bothering to hide her grin.

I glance into the living room, where my son is playing with his future twin cousins. They already have tons of toys out, but my parents don't seem to mind. In fact, they usually stand by, watching fondly, while the kids practically tear up the house. They're definitely a lot more relaxed when it comes to grandkids than they were with their own children.

"So what are the plans tonight?" she asks, leading me into the kitchen for a few minutes.

"I'm going to meet Grayson and Laken at Pony Up. They offered to pick me up, but it's such a gorgeous night, I don't mind walking. It's only two blocks."

"Probably a smart move, and I'm sure Gray will drop you off at your place when you leave," she says, grabbing two bottles of water from the fridge and sliding one across the counter. "Or...you could get a ride from someone else." She wiggles her eyebrows suggestively, causing a bubble of laughter to spill from my lips.

"Subtle," I mumble, shaking my head.

"So? What's going on with you and Malcolm Wright?" she asks, leaning against the counter.

I sigh, not really sure how to answer this. After that big, long text thread a week ago, we've only seen each other Thursday night at his place. We've texted a few times, but they were casual and friendly. "To be honest, I'm not sure. I guess I consider him a friend. He's been great with Trace and took him fishing while I was cleaning his house, which you know. And besides, I'm not really sure I'm looking for a relationship right now. I need to focus on Trace."

"There's nothing wrong with focusing on your son *and* on yourself, Leni."

I nod, not really sure what more to say. I guess I'll cross that bridge if anything more were to transpire between us, but I'm not really sure anything will. Malcolm has been polite, friendly, and maybe even a little flirty at times—but that's who he is. He's never taken it any further than that.

"Have you heard from Greg lately?"

She hit another sore spot right on the head. "No."

Mom shakes her head and tsks. "Such a shame he turned out to be a complete turd."

Her comment catches me by surprise, and I can't stop from laughing. "You're correct. He's a complete turd."

She grins and reaches for my hand, giving it a light squeeze. "You're doing a wonderful job raising him, honey. Don't ever doubt that."

I swallow over the sudden lump in my throat. "Thanks. How's Dad getting around?"

"Oh, he's fine. He stopped using that crutch a few days ago, which was probably for the better. He was going to kill himself sooner or later," she says with a laugh. "It still gets just a little sore on him, but as long as he takes it easy and rests, he's fine."

I'm just glad it wasn't any worse than a bad sprain.

"Now, go get ready to meet your sister. They should be about finished with dinner by now and headed up to the bar. I've heard that Tucker guy play, and he puts on a great show," my mom says, referring to Tucker Simms, a Mason Creek transplant who moved here from Billings. He plays at all the town festivals and events, with his mix of classic country and 90's hits.

"Night, Mom. Call me if you need me," I reiterate, even though I don't need to. I know they'll be fine.

"Go. You kids have fun," she demands, practically pushing me out the door.

I say goodbye to Trace and the girls and head out the door. I've never been one to go out a lot, especially when I was back in Washington, but now that I'm home, I admit I'm enjoying getting to see friends every now and again.

And I know Trace is in good hands.

Let the night begin.

Pony Up is packed, but that's to be expected with Tucker playing. He knows how to draw an audience. Even in the crowded bar, it's easy to spot my sister's vibrant red hair. I was always jealous of her hair color growing up, having to settle of the dull brown I was born with.

"You're here," Laken bellows, the slight flush to her cheeks telling me she's already had a drink or two.

I hug my sister and am greeted by everyone already there. Justine is here, who's with Tucker, Grady, and Charlee, as well as a few others I've come to be reacquainted with since my return. "Where's Grayson?" I ask, glancing around for my sister's other half.

"He's grabbing a few drinks at the bar," she says, and something about the Cheshire cat grin sets me on high alert.

"What?" I ask, narrowing my skeptical hazel eyes at her.

"Oh, nothing!" she sings, smiling over her straw as she sucks up the last of whatever was in her glass. "You look ah-may-zing," she adds, giving me a look from head to toe.

I didn't exactly put a lot of effort into tonight's appearance, but I didn't just pull my hair up and throw on a T-shirt either. My hair is down, straightened with the flat iron I rarely use, and I decided to wear some of the clothes in the back of my closet I only pull out on the rarest occasions. I'm wearing a pair of cutoff shorts, and while I don't usually don things that might accentuate my ass, these shorts are stretchier than normal denim and do well at concealing my rolls. The top I chose is a deep blue halter top with little white flowers all over it. Plus, it's super breezy and flowy and doesn't make me feel like I'm on display. I learned a long time ago, with boobs as ginormous as mine, V-necks are not my friend. Unless you want every guy within a two-mile radius ogling your girls.

"Hey, Leni." I turn and offer Grayson a smile as he hands my sister another drink.

That's when I spot the man standing beside him, holding a beer bottle in each hand. "Hi," Malcolm says, handing me a drink.

"Hi," I reply, the word coming out a nervous squeak.

Malcolm lifts his beer to his lips and winks, sending my heart beating into a level that would certainly concern most physicians.

Fortunately for me, my sister pulls me into a conversation with Justine, and soon The Tucker Simms Band is starting to play. The girls instantly pull me into the middle of the dance floor, where I try to hide closer to the band so I'm not directly in anyone's line of sight. Their popular rendition of "Sweet Home Alabama" kicks things off and flows directly into some John Michael Montgomery.

After the third song ends, I wave my hand over my face, desperately needing a drink to cool down. As I approach the table, pulling money from my wristlet, I'm surprised to see Malcolm there, holding out another beer.

I take the bottle and give him a suspicious glance. "You didn't roofie this, did you?" I tease.

He snorts out a quick laugh. "I don't need to drug you to get in your pants, Lenora." He leans closer and whispers in my ear, "All I'd have to do is turn on my charms."

I dramatically roll my eyes. "Your charms? Is that some cheesy pickup line?" I ask, taking a drink of the cold brew.

"Cheesy?" He gasps, feigning shock. "I'll have you know my pickup lines are the best." He turns serious and leans in. "Are you a parking ticket, because you have *fine* written all over you."

I burst out laughing, catching the attention of everyone around me.

"Not that one? How about? Are you a camera? Because every time I look at you I smile."

I try to cover my giggles with my hand, which only makes him grin more.

"What about this one? If your phone number was a dollar amount, what would it be?"

I groan and shake my head. "Those are horrible!"

He tsks. "Ladies these days don't know good lines," he declares to Grayson, who's now standing beside him.

Grayson gives me a shocked look. "You mean you don't like, there's something wrong with my cell phone. It doesn't have your number in it."

I giggle and shake my head. "You're lucky my sister already loves you."

He seems to sober a bit, his eyes seeking her out. "Yes, I am."

"Come on, you've had enough of a break," Justine says, pulling on my arm.

I go to set my bottle down, but Malcolm snatches it up. "I'll hold it for you."

With a quick flash of a smile, I'm pulled back out into the thick of the dance floor for a few more songs.

The night progresses in a fit of laughter, drinks, and more fun than I anticipated. And to my surprise, a lot of flirting. Malcolm's a natural flirt, but I've found I enjoy the banter with him. I've even shocked myself with some of the things I've said to him over the course of the evening.

Since I walked here, I decide to have one more drink. It's getting late, though Tucker still has another hour to play, and even though the streets of Mason Creek are safe, I prefer to have a clearer mind when making my way home.

I head for the bar, having finished my previous drink before hitting the dance floor and chatting with my friends. I'm able to slip between a few patrons and catch the bartender's attention. Just as he steps up, I feel a presence behind me. I already know who it is without turning around. It's as if I can feel him, as if my body is hyperaware of his.

One half recognizing the other.

I don't know if it's the alcohol flowing through my veins or the flirtatious banter, but I sway my hips and rock back on my heels, my ass coming in contact with the man standing behind me. Malcolm leans forward, pressing his front to my back, as he rests his palm on the counter beside me.

To those around me, it looks like a man leaning forward to order a drink.

To me, it's a man making it known how badly he desires a woman.

Because, even though it's been a while for me, there's no doubt in my mind Malcolm wants me. The erection that brushed against my body is the first indication. The other is the look in his eyes when I glance over my shoulder. It's raw, hungry, and makes me shiver in anticipation.

"One more, please," Malcolm states to the bartender without removing his gaze from me.

A few seconds later, a fresh beer bottle in the brand I've been drinking all night is placed in front of me, and before I can pull cash from the wristlet attached to my arm, money is exchanged.

I take the drink and turn to face the man who has bought every single drink I've had this evening.

"Thank you, but I'm fully capable of purchasing my own beer."

"I'm well aware, Lenora. Having a good evening?" he asks as we step away from the bar to allow others to place orders.

"I am, thanks. You?" I bring my bottle to my lips and take a drink and notice how his gaze follows my movements.

"I am. The view has been...incredible." He has the softest smile on his lips, one that makes him look incredibly kissable.

Maybe I don't need any more to drink...

"Hey!" Laken hollers, throwing her arm around my waist.

I grin instantly. "I love drunk Laken. She's so fun," I tell my sister.

"No more to drink! The last time I drank too much, you let Gray carry me up the stairs, and I smelled him!" my sister declares, her glassy eyes narrowing into little slits.

"Yes, but if I had left it up to you, you'd still be a lovesick puppy staring at him from the corner of the room, too afraid to make a move. I still wish I had recorded it," I tease, glancing to Malcolm. "It was the best."

Laken hits me on the arm. Not hard, but still. "You're mean."

I giggle, which causes her to giggle. Then Justine and Charlee join us and start laughing too.

"What are they laughing about?" Grayson asks Malcolm.

Malcolm just shakes his head and hollers over the music, "Not sure, and I'm pretty sure none of them know either."

Just then, a slow ballad begins, and we all start swaying to the music. "I love this song," Justine says.

"Me too. Come on, Grayson," Laken requests, reaching out her hand for the man she loves. He takes it, kisses the top of her knuckles, and leads her to the dance floor. I can't help but swoon just a bit, as he takes my sister to the dance floor and pulls her close. I'm so grateful they have each other. I know it wasn't easy for him, taking the chance on love a second time, especially after losing his first wife, but I'm so happy he did.

My sister has never been happier.

Charlee and Grady walk out next, followed by a whole slew of other couples. Justine remains at my side, since Tucker's a little busy singing, as does Malcolm.

Suddenly, a young woman pushes her way between us and practically throws herself at Malcolm. "Come on, Malcolm. Let's dance," she slurs, clearly a tad bit tipsy.

"Sorry, darlin', but I don't dance." He throws her a wink before bringing his beer to his lips and gazing out at the growing dancing crowd.

"Awww," she pouts, literally jutting out her heavily painted bottom lip. "Well, if dancing isn't your thing, we could always go hang out elsewhere." The way she practically coos as she strokes his arm lets anyone within hearing distance know exactly what she means.

A wave of nausea hits me, the beer suddenly not sitting well in my gut.

I look away quickly, wishing I weren't standing right here. I mean, Malcolm is free to do whatever—or whoever—he wants to do, right? He's single, and I have no claim on him whatsoever. Yet, it feels like someone punched me in the stomach as I picture him going off with this girl.

The jealousy is real, and I don't like it.

I'm just about to excuse myself, to go anywhere but here, but am stopped in my tracks with his next words.

"You know, I think I will dance," he says, the deep, sexy timbre of his voice sending my stomach straight down to my toes. He holds out his hand, but not in her direction.

I glance down, shocked to see it in front of me.

"Lenora, shall we?"

Chapter THIRTEEN

Malcolm

She looks at my hand as if it were a snake about to bite her. Her stunned hazel eyes finally move up to meet mine, and it feels like I'm struck by lightning. I'm so fucking drawn to her it's not funny, but I know this connection is more than just attraction. There's this deep-down longing to get to know her better, and not just on a physical level.

Though, that desire level is pretty strong too.

Completely ignoring the woman in front of me, I take Lenora's beer and set it on the closest table. Then, I take her hand in my own and lead her to the dance floor. I can feel eyes on me, no doubt about it, but I don't care. Let them talk.

When I pull her into my arms and draw her close, it feels too right. Even though she's much shorter than me, our bodies align perfectly.

For dancing.

And other things too...

We dance in perfect rhythm, but I already knew we would. I watched the way she moved all night, her hips swaying to the beat, her body moving as if it were made for dancing. I've been completely enthralled—and maybe a little hard—since the first time she took the floor, trying to hide behind her friends.

After a few minutes, the song rolls into a second slow song, and I almost turn around and tell Tucker thank you. I'm not ready to let go of her yet. I feel her shift closer, her hands gripping the back of my shirt. Leni rests her cheek on my chest and sighs. I can feel her pressed firmly against me, and fuck, if I don't really like it.

A lot.

"You're a pretty good dancer for someone who can't dance." I glance down, meeting her curious gaze.

"I didn't say I can't dance; I just don't do it."

"Why?" she asks, keeping perfect time to the beat.

I take a breath, inhaling the sweet scent of her shampoo. Her hair is down and straight, my fingers itch to slide through the soft strands. "It's just not my thing."

"Maybe you're worried about having two left feet," she teases, wrinkling her nose as she grins.

"Maybe I just haven't had the right partner."

The humor slowly falls from her face as she gazes up at me. The need to kiss her has never been stronger than it is right now. I find myself leaning forward, my lips seeking hers out, needing to taste them.

She tips her chin and licks her lips as she goes up on her tiptoes. Just before we meet in the middle, I hear a loud gasp to my immediate right. The noise startles both of us, and we jolt back.

"Oh, you were about to kiss!" Laken bellows, her eyes wide with drunken excitement.

"Yeah, thanks for that, Lake."

"Did I spoil it?" she asks, just as the song ends, and to be honest, I'm not sure if I'm grateful or upset. The fact that I almost kissed Leni here, in a packed bar, is probably not my smartest move. I'm usually much smoother than that. But on the other hand, I really wanted to kiss her, even if it's in the middle of Pony Up and will result in front page gossip talk by morning.

Leni just shakes her head at her sister and drops her arms. I miss them instantly. A new song starts up, this one much more upbeat, and as we step off the floor, I feel her hand brush against my leg. My entire body is alive and hot, like a volcano slowly spreading through my veins.

"Leni and Malcolm almost kissed!" Laken announced to the girls the moment we get back to the small table we've been occupying.

"Almost?" Justine asks, her eyes wide.

A blush creeps up Leni's neck as she tries to hide behind her hair. "Let's not talk about it," she insists, grabbing her drink and taking a long pull.

All of the women, well, except for Leni, turn to me and give a simultaneous, "Aww."

I can't help but laugh as I shake my head. "I'll be back, ladies," I say, excusing myself to use the restroom.

Of course, on the way, I run into several people who want to stop and chat. Good thing I don't really have to use the bathroom. It was an excuse to step away for a few minutes and clear my head. Being so close to her, especially after holding her in my arms, is giving me all sorts of ideas about how I want this night to end, and if I'm being honest with myself, I don't want to rush it with her. Usually, I'd flirt and make my intentions known, but with Leni, I'm taking a different approach.

It takes much longer for me to return to the group I've been hanging with all night, and as I approach where the ladies are gathered, I'm surprised by their conversation.

"Really? You've never had one?" Justine gapes across the group, directly at Leni, catching my attention.

"Come on, you guys. I was with Greg on and off since college, and before that, there was only a totally drunk guy at a frat party and Tony back in high school, and kissing him was like having my face licked by a dog," Leni replies, making the girls giggle.

"You knew with Grayson though, right?" Charlee asks Laken, who's already nodding.

"I totally knew. Our first kiss was quick, but it was the sweetest. Gray asked me if he could kiss me, and I said yes. It was…perfect," Laken replies, her voice all syrupy and far-off.

"Aww," the others fuss together.

"I can't believe you've never had an epic kiss," Charlee states, all eyes on Leni.

Laken just gapes at her sister. "How is this possible?"

She shrugs. "I don't know, I guess I've just never really thought about it. Greg was…he was comfortable."

"But he never blew your socks off," Justine deduces.

I watch as Leni shakes her head. I think about all the kisses I've had—and yes, I've had my fair share of them—but quickly realize, while some have been pretty damn good, I wouldn't consider any of them epic. Kissing was always a prelude to sex. It was enjoyable, yet necessary to get to the next step. I have never kissed a woman just for the sake of kissing her, mostly because I always knew it was leading somewhere.

But staring at Leni, seeing the disappointment on her face at never experiencing a great kiss, makes me yearn for more. To show her just how fucking beautiful, how fucking worthy she is. And the

Perfect Kiss

weirdest part? I don't even care about the "next step." Sure, I'd love to get naked with her, but that's not all I want. I want her to always think about me the next time she's asked about epic kisses.

I want to be hers.

My feet are moving before I can stop myself. I slip easily between those around her and step directly in front of Leni. My hands thread into her soft hair as her eyes widen in surprise. I don't think. Hell, I don't even think I breathe. I give her a split second to stop me before I take her lips with my own.

The moment we touch, it's like…magic.

Gasps echo around me, but then they suddenly fade away as I slowly deepen the kiss. The room is suddenly silent as she moves against my mouth, her hands gripping my shirt at my sides. She tastes as sweet as honey. Her lips are like sin, ripe and made for kissing.

I want more.

My tongue slides along the seam of her mouth, and the moment it opens, I delve inside, tasting, savoring, and quickly realizing I could kiss this woman forever and never get enough.

When I finally rip my lips from hers, we both suck in a greedy breath of oxygen. I crack open my eyes to see hers still closed and her lips all swollen and enticing. I'm a nanosecond away from starting the kiss all over again when she faintly whispers, "Wow."

"Wow is right. Holy crap, that was hot." Laken's words slowly permeate the lust-filled fog in my brain.

Leni opens her eyes, and the moment they focus on me, she softly smiles. Then as quick as that smile appears, it's ripped away. Those hazel orbs widen in shock as she looks around. "Holy shit," she mumbles as a blush creeps up her neck. Those delicate little fingers that were once gripping my shirt are now touching her cheeks, trying to cool the heat of her embarrassment.

Knowing I need to say something, I step forward and lower my mouth to her ear. Instantly, I can smell the sweetness of her hair, which only kicks up the desire to kiss her once more. "Holy shit is right. Best. Kiss. Ever," I murmur just loud enough for her to hear over the noise of the bar.

She turns those startled eyes my way and grins. "Epic."

"I'm pretty sure every cell phone in the place was pointed at you two," Justine says over the rim of her glass.

"Great, just what I needed," Leni grumbles with an eye roll.

I should feel bad about that, because of me, she'll be the talk of the town for the foreseeable future, but I can't seem to find the gumption to get too worked up. Not after that kiss. It will forever be burned into my memory, the kiss I would forever compare all other kisses to.

But I don't care. I've never experienced anything like that, and all I want is to do it again.

And again...

I stay close to her but let her do her thing as the night winds down. Our sides brush against each other as we visit with friends, and I can't stop the desire that swirls in my gut as her soft hair tickles my arm. All I can think about was how it felt to have it threaded between my fingers as I kissed her.

Once last call is offered, our small group starts to dissipate. I wave goodbye to the others yet remain very near to Leni. I know she walked here, but I want to be the one to take her home. No, I *need* to be the one.

"Do you want a ride?" her sister asks as she threads her arms around Grayson. There's no missing the way her gaze moves from Leni to me, as if looking for confirmation that I'm taking her home.

"No, I'm okay to walk. You two enjoy the rest of your kid-free night."

Laken looks up at me, as if seeking confirmation her sister will get home safely, to which I nod in agreement. No way am I letting her just walk home. Even in a safe town like Mason Creek, I'm not leaving it to chance. Plus, I'd rather have her in my car, and maybe in my arms once more before the night is through. I'd definitely be okay with replaying that kiss.

"Night," Laken says, pulling her older sister into a quick hug. She turns to me next and wraps her arms around my shoulders. "Please be good to her," she whispers just loud enough for only my ears to hear.

A sobering feeling slides through my veins. Leni's been jacked around by her ex for years, and the last thing I want is to do the same. I've never been a relationship guy, but I wasn't lying when I told her in those texts that I want to try.

Sooner, rather than later.

"Ready?" I ask as Leni sets her empty bottle down on the closest table.

She looks at me curiously. "I'm okay to walk."

I nod, completely prepared for a rebuttal. "I know you are, but why walk when I'm perfectly capable of driving you home?"

Her eyes fill with skepticism. "You drank too."

"I did," I start, placing my hand on her lower back and guiding her through the busy bar, "but I only had two drinks hours ago. I've been drinking water since." I notice several probing sets of eyes following us as we push through the door and step out into the warm summer night, but I ignore them and the questions they ask.

She stops on the sidewalk, making sure we're out of the way from others leaving. "But I literally live right there," she says, pointing to where the laundromat sits a block and a half away.

I step forward, leaning in close. "I know, but if you walk, I won't be able to steal another kiss before I say goodnight."

Leni smiles, her features softening with the simplest of gestures. "Okay. Thank you."

Leading her to my car, I keep my hand on her back and escort her. She slips onto the buttery-soft leather seats easily, and I can't help but watch how her palm gently glides over the material. It makes me wish her hand was rubbing something else…

We're both quiet as I drive to where she lives, wishing it wouldn't be so weird to take a longer route. Moments later, I'm pulling into the back where her car is parked and stopping beside the door. "Wait for me." Jumping out, I move to the passenger door and hold it open, trying to be the perfect gentleman.

"Thanks." Even under the dim security light, I can see the blush on her cheeks.

As we slowly approach the rear entrance of her building, I reach for her hand. Leni steps up on the single concrete step at her door and turns to face me. She's still not quite to my height, but it raises her enough to the right goodnight kiss level.

"What are you plans tomorrow?" I ask, stepping forward until we're almost chest to chest.

"Oh, well, I'll have to pick Trace up from my parents' house after breakfast, and we usually do our grocery shopping at some point. Why?"

I link our fingers and meet those intoxicating hazel eyes. "I was going to see if you'd like to hang out with me tomorrow, and I knew you'd probably have Trace, since he was with your parents tonight. I thought maybe we could all go fishing or maybe out to my grandparents' place. We can fish in their pond and ride a four-wheeler around their property."

"I don't know how to ride a four-wheeler," she confesses.

"You don't have to know how unless you want to learn. We can take their four-seater UTV. It even has seat belts for Champ." It's weird for me to say that. I've never been concerned about safety features like belts before, but in the short time I've known Lenora, I know it's important and something she'd want to know to ensure her son's safety.

"Okay."

I instantly smile. "Yeah?"

She nods and returns my grin. "Yes."

I move forward just a whisper, until I'm almost touching her. "Can I kiss you goodnight?"

"I'd be sad if you didn't," she murmurs, tilting her head upward.

As I lean down, she closes her eyes, but I leave mine open. I want to see her face while I claim her mouth with my own. Her lips are so eager, so pliant against mine it's hard to not deepen it or take it farther. But I don't.

At least not tonight.

Instead, I watch her eyelids flutter and how little crinkles appear across her forehead. I never thought I'd find anything like it sexy, but I do. So much.

Threading my fingers into her hair, I hold her head and finally truly give in to the kiss. Closing my eyes, I indulge, taste, and savor the feel of her mouth and the way her body arches into mine. If I'm not careful, I could easily fall into the abyss of wanting more.

Reluctantly, I pull away, only to find her lips just as swollen and damp as earlier tonight when I kissed her at the bar. A groan slips through my lips and my cock aches in my pants. Fuck, I really want this woman.

She opens her eyes and blinks, as if clearing away the fog. Finally, she smiles, and my heart feels like it's going to rip from my chest.

"Goodnight, Lenora," I whisper, grudgingly removing my hands from her hair and taking a step back. "I'll text you in the morning, okay? We can decide what time to go."

"Okay."

I brush my lips across hers once more, because I've discovered I'm a very weak man when it comes to her, before turning around and returning to my car. If I don't drive away now, I won't at all. I'll take her upstairs and do every single dirty thing I've been dreaming about, but that's not how I want this to go.

Not with her.

I wait until she slips inside and makes sure the door is locked before I start the engine and back away. Only when I'm about to head for home do I look up and find her standing at a window. When our eyes meet, she holds up a hand in a wave before touching her lips.

"Fuck, you're in trouble," I mumble as I finally pull away, trying to adjust my tight pants as I go. "Big, big trouble."

Chapter FOURTEEN

Leni

"Trace, are you ready?" I holler, checking my watch for the umpteenth time since we got home from my parents' house.

"Ready!" he proclaims, running from his room in a pair of jeans and cowboy boots.

Not what I laid out for him.

"What are you wearing?" I ask, making sure there's snacks packed in the bookbag I'm taking with fresh clothes for Trace, a few juice boxes, and things he can eat if he gets hungry.

"My boots! Papa says they're good for fishing. We're going fishing, right?" he asks, his eager, hopeful eyes meeting mine.

"We are," I confirm, checking the bag one more time.

Earlier, I had barely returned home from retrieving Trace when the text came from Malcolm. He still wanted to take us fishing and riding at his grandparents' homestead just outside of town, and we made the plan to leave at one. That gave us the entire afternoon to enjoy our outing.

Just then, a knock sounds on the downstairs outside door. "Just a minute," I holler before turning to my son. "Grab your tennis shoes too, just in case."

When he takes off for his bedroom, I go down the stairs to unlock the door. Malcolm looks freshly showered and smells amazing. He's wearing a light-colored T-shirt that hugs his upper arms and chest, well-worn blue jeans, and a pair of cowboy boots. Plus, a ball cap. I never thought they were sexy until I saw one on top of his head.

He looks positively edible.

"Keep looking at me like that and we'll never make it to my grandparents' place," he mumbles.

"Sorry," I state quickly, clearing my throat and the memory of our shared kisses from my brain.

Okay, let's not go that far. There's no way I'll be forgetting those kisses anytime soon.

He steps forward, bends down, and slides his lips against mine. "You look beautiful," he whispers before pulling the door closed behind him.

I glance down, taking in my fitted T-shirt, black shorts, and old sneakers. My hair is pulled through the back of a ball cap and I'm not wearing any makeup. "Mess is probably more accurate."

Malcolm tsks and shakes his head. He leans down, somehow avoiding the clash of our hats, and kisses me on the lips. "Stunning," he whispers before standing to his full height. "Where's Trace?"

"Here! And ready," my son exclaims, practically running down the stairs to join us.

"Let me grab my bag and keys. I'll be right back."

I triple check the bag before I finally concede I have everything, including a small baggy of first aid items. When I return downstairs, I find Malcolm and Trace already outside. Trace is telling Malcolm all about his sleepover with the girls last night, but I'm struck by the image they create. There, standing in the gravel, is a man and my son. They're both wearing jeans, T-shirts, and boots, and while their features are completely different, it's their mannerisms that catch my eye. The way they both have their arms crossed over their chests, Malcolm's as he listens intently and Trace's as he mimics the man in front of him.

I want my son to have this.

To have someone he can look up to and copy. Someone to teach him all the manly things a father can teach—the things I can't.

Malcolm looks my way and smiles, the sweetest, most serene grin I've ever witnessed. It makes his harder features...soft. The bossy man in the council chambers and the courtroom is a big teddy bear. Completely adorable and...loveable.

No.

Not going there.

I clear my throat and jump in the first moment Trace takes a pause in his story. "Ready!" The word comes out all high and squeaky.

Malcolm arches an eyebrow but opens both the passenger side doors on his car. "Trace and I already grabbed his seat from your car."

"All right."

I don't have an opportunity to help Trace into the car and buckle, since Malcolm is right there taking care of it. When I go ahead and sit in the front seat, I hear Trace ask, "What's that?"

I glance over my shoulder as Malcolm answers, "That's a picnic for later. We can eat dinner where we're going. That okay, Champ?"

"Do you have peanut butter and jelly sandwiches?" my little one asks.

Malcolm gasps. "I do! I hope you like grape jelly."

"It's my favorite jelly!"

"Excellent," Malcolm replies with a chuckle. "Watch yourself. I'm gonna shut the door."

He comes around to the driver's door while I try to swallow down the bubble of emotion that's suddenly lodged in my throat, restricting my airways. The ride to his grandparents' place is short, but I'm so grateful for Trace's constant talking, because I'm not sure I could right now. I keep thinking about the kiss and how it made me feel, as well as the overwhelming vibes I get when I see Malcolm with my son. It's too much, and I don't know how to process it.

We pull down a long, winding lane that leads back to a gorgeous home. "My grandparents built this place after my grandpa retired from being mayor. He inherited the land from his father but waited to build the house until he was done serving the citizens of Mason Creek. He did dig the pond and kept up the property early on though. Grandma planted all those trees and flowering shrubs when I was a young boy. I fell out of that big oak tree there and broke my arm when I was four."

I look at the large tree he pointed to and can practically see why a young boy would have been so interested in climbing it. It's the perfect climbing tree, with low, wide branches and lots of cover.

Malcolm drives down the lane, continuing past the large house and garage. He follows the path back to the pond and parks in a large mowed grassy area. "Ready?" he asks Trace when he shuts off the vehicle.

"Yes!" My son already has his buckles released and is reaching for the door handle before anyone can tell him to get out.

The sun is hot, but the view is simply stunning. The mountains look amazing in the distance behind a fairly big body of water and a massive, wooded piece of land. There's a dock that extends out into the pond, as well as a decent-sized building off to the side. There are trees to provide shady spots and even a sandy area at the water's edge for a beach with brightly painted Adirondack chairs.

It's a great place. Quiet and inviting.

I turn to help Malcolm unload his trunk, and before I can holler at Trace to stay away from the water, he's already gone. "Hey, Champ, don't get too close until you have your life jacket on, okay?"

"'Kay!" he yells, returning to where we are to help unload today's goodies. I grab the insulated bag from the back seat and smile when I see both of their arms loaded up with gear. I've always enjoyed fishing; even when I was a kid. My dad used to take me and my sister to the lake on weekends, and his insistent desire to wet a line stuck with me. My sister, not so much. She used to go, but always preferred reading at the water's edge or on the boat.

We head for the dock and deposit our load under a shade tree. While Trace wiggles into his life jacket, Malcolm works to bait the small hook on the Spider-Man pole. "My grandpa stocks the pond every five years or so. There should be plenty to catch."

"Can we keep 'em?" Trace asks, eager to cast.

"If they're big enough. We'll clean and put them in salty ice water overnight," Malcolm replies, handing the baited pole to my son.

"Can we have 'em for dinner?"

Malcolm chuckles and leads him down to the edge of the dock. "No, not tonight. We're having our picnic, remember?"

"Yes! With the good jelly."

"That's right. Do you want to cast?" he says, stepping back so he doesn't get hooked, yet close enough he can jump in and help if he needs to.

"I got it." And he does. Trace throws a pretty decent cast and sets the line. "Tomorrow?" he asks, clearly still thinking about eating the fish he plans to catch.

"Well, tomorrow night I have meetings. I'm done by six on Wednesday, though. What about you guys?" Malcolm asks, crouching down beside Trace.

"Mom? Do you have to work then?" he hollers, barely glancing away from where his bobber bounces in the water.

"My last client is at five, so I should be done by six thirty," I reply, walking out to join them on the dock.

"Can we cook the fish with Malcolm?" he asks, his hopeful eyes pleading with me to say yes.

I glance at the man beside him, who just shrugs. "Well, maybe. You start school this week, and we were going to plan early bedtimes, remember?"

"Oh," he replies, dropping his head for a brief moment. "Oh, yeah!" he adds, realizing he's finally going to start kindergarten.

Malcolm goes and grabs one of the other fishing poles and baits the hook. He brings it over and hands it to me. "You know how to cast this thing?"

"Are you kidding me?" I quip, narrowing my eyes. "I'm practically pro-level."

Malcolm snorts. "Well, let's see it, Kevin VanDam," he teases, referring to the successful Bassmaster fisherman.

It's been a few years since I've done this, but it's like riding a bike, right? I press the release button, position the pole at my shoulder like I used to, and let it fly. Only the hook and bait go straight down with a slap.

Trace giggles as Malcolm shakes his head and reaches for the pole. "Need a hand, Kevin?"

"No," I argue, reeling in the line and getting ready once again. "I can do this."

This time, when I throw the line and release the button, it soars across the sky and lands with a satisfying plop out in the pond.

"Not bad," Malcolm states proudly before grabbing the third and final pole, baiting, and casting it with precision and expertise.

We all take a seat on the dock, our feet dangling near the water. Because of the summer heat and very little rain, the pond appears a little lower than normal, judging by the lines of foliage and dirt around the perimeter.

I glance over and watch Trace as he concentrates on the task at hand. His bobber moves, causing him to get ready. Just as it dips below the surface, he yanks up and starts to reel. It's entertaining watching him and Malcolm work together, one spinning the Spider-Man reel while the other coaches him along. Malcolm runs and grabs the net, dipping it into the water and pulling a decent sized bluegill out of the pond.

"Look at that!" my son proclaims.

"Hold the line," Malcolm instructs, pulling out his phone and snapping a photo.

My heart melts seeing the giddiness and toothless smile on his face.

"Look, Mom! I did it all by myself," he announces, as they carefully set the fish on the dock.

Malcolm works to remove the hook, with Trace bending down and taking in his every move. Once it's free, the older of the two announces that it's the prefect size to keep, so my son runs over to grab the live trap to tie on the dock. It'll keep the fish alive yet contained until we're finished.

They bait the hook a second time, cast it into the pond, and take a seat, side by side. Trace glances up, squinting against the sun, and smiles at Malcolm. He looks down and returns the grin, only to remove his ball cap from his head, tighten the strap in back, and place it on my son's head. Trace reaches up and adjusts it, offering another toothy grin and a happy, "Thanks."

That's how we spend the next hour and a half, catching fish and adding them to our catch trap. When we have enough for more than one meal, Malcolm announces it's time to go for a ride around the property. Before Trace can take off in his excitement, he helps clean up the fishing gear and takes it over to the tree.

Then, he's practically running right alongside Malcolm as he goes to the small building and removes a padlock. Inside, there's a four-seater MULE UTV, and the moment the door is rolled open, Trace jumps onto the seat.

"Come here," Malcolm instructs, picking him up and setting him on his lap.

I stand back and watch as he starts the UTV, slowly pulls it out of the building, and heads my way. The look on Trace's face says it all. He's completely beside himself with excitement as he holds the wheel, helping Malcolm steer.

"Can I drive?" my son asks, making both adults laugh.

"Do you have a driver's license?" Malcolm asks in a teasing tone.

"No, silly, I'm five."

"Then, I'm afraid you can't drive. However, you can sit beside me in a seat belt. Deal?"

Trace shrugs and moves to the other seat. "Okay."

"Ready?" Malcolm asks, reaching over and pushing a strand of hair that fell from my ball cap behind my ear. The way the sunlight hits his face, I can see the dark stubble from the day really coming through. I wonder if it's coarse or soft, and my fingers itch to find out.

"Maybe you two should go," I reply, staying right where I am, a bit nervous to ride that big utility vehicle.

"I won't go fast, I promise. Not with you and Champ on board. You'll enjoy it," he insists, his finger lingering on my cheek just a touch longer than expected.

With a quick nod, I hop in the back seat and buckle my safety belt too.

We cruise around the property, following trails in the dirt and grass. Malcolm points out several areas to Trace, including markings on a tree where deer have been scratching to shed antlers. After another hour, we wind our way back to where we started and put the UTV away. When Malcolm and Trace return from the shed, they have a blanket and spread it on the ground under the big oak tree.

As Malcolm sets out the food, involving Trace's help, I can't get over the fact this is a date. Not just any date, but a great date. Never have I been asked to include Trace. With Greg, it was always drive-thru dinners, and on the rare occasion we'd find a sitter for our young son, he always wanted to go to the bar and hang out with his friends. Eventually, it turned into just him going.

Now, here we are, our first official date, and my son is an active, prominent part of it. As a single mom, that means more to me than any fancy dinner I could have been taken to. The fact he kept it casual and to the things my child likes to do speaks volumes for the man himself.

"So, Champ, when you take a woman out on a date, you have to make sure you treat her special. And your mom is special," he says, placing the first sandwich container in front of me. "You always serve the lady first or allow her to order first at a restaurant. It's the gentlemanly thing to do."

Trace nods, hanging on Malcolm's every word. "But girls are gross!"

We get a good chuckle at Trace's candor. "Well, I, too, once thought girls were yucky, but I promise you, you'll eventually change your mind. Girls are pretty great," he replies, looking up and winking at me.

Trace makes sure to give me grapes first, even though I can tell he's ready to dive into his own food, but he heeds Malcolm's words. When the food is finally distributed, he looks up at Malcolm, as if asking for permission to eat. "Go ahead. I hope you like the PB&J. Made it myself," he boasts proudly.

He does, diving in with both hands, and it gives Malcolm and me an opportunity to quietly eat and visit. "Have you always wanted to be mayor and an attorney?" I ask, popping a grape into my mouth.

Malcolm nods and swallows his bite. "Always. I watched my grandpa and dad succeed in both the courtroom and the council chambers. I took in everything, thriving on their work and determination to make Mason Creek a better place. I knew at a young age I wanted to do that too. I was elected the youngest mayor in town history, less than a year ago, and have loved it."

"That's amazing," I reply between bites of my sandwich. "If I had been what I wanted to be when I was a young girl, I'd be a dolphin trainer right now."

He laughs, that deep, rich sound so soothing and sexy. "Not a lot of dolphins in Montana."

"Definitely not. Even in high school, I had no clue. I picked accounting because I enjoyed math, but turns out, it wasn't the job for me. And cleaning is...I don't know. Fun? Everyone thinks I'm weird to actually enjoy it, but I do."

"Who cares what everyone else thinks?" he asks, meeting my gaze.

Perfect Kiss

I consider his question and realize I don't. Not really. This place is a small town and yes, everyone knows everything about you, usually moments after it happens, but it doesn't really matter to me.

"I always thought my future was to serve on a bigger stage," he says, pulling me away from my own thoughts. "Governor, maybe? Senator? I was never sure which but knew that's where my road would lead me. Now, I guess I'm finding my niche here. Maybe a small town isn't so bad, you know? It has some of the best things to offer in life. Some of the most amazing people are here."

When he looks at me, there's something very settling in his eyes. As if he's discovered there's more to life than work or big political dreams. Maybe I'm looking too much into it, but it's as if he's found something worth staying for. "That's a very bold and admirable goal."

He gives a weird nod, shrug thing, but doesn't say anything more on the subject. Instead, he gives me a big grin and whispers, "Admirable enough for a goodnight kiss?"

I can't stop the giggle as I pop a grape into my mouth. Slowly, I chew and smile. "Maybe."

Chapter FIFTEEN

Malcolm

Maybe.

I've been thinking about that one word since it fell from her lips.

After dinner, we visited for a little longer while Trace played in the sand before packing everything up and loading my car. On the ride to her place, I listened to Trace talk animatedly about the fish he caught, all while holding her hand on the console. I can't get enough of that kid.

Now, I'm pulling into the parking area where her car sits to drop them off.

And I don't want to.

I want to hang out.

Be with them.

Breathe in their energy and light.

As I stop my car, everyone seems a little slower to get out. Even Leni, who had a big list of things to do yet tonight, drags her feet. Outside, I open the trunk and start handing things to Trace that will stay here. When I get to the life jacket, I ask, "Do you want to keep it here or store it in my shed?"

He seems to consider his options, giving considerable thought to his choices. "Your place. Then it'll be there when I go fishing again."

I nod in agreement and set the vest back inside.

"What about the fishies?" he asks, pointing to the cooler that contains today's catches.

"Well, I'll get them filleted and cleaned up. I know you have an earlier bedtime for school, so what if I bring them over Wednesday and cook you dinner like we discussed the other day?" I offer, the idea just coming to me. Really, it's a win-win. I get to see Trace and Leni in the middle of a busy week, even for just a little bit.

Which reminds me...

"We need to discuss your work schedule," I say, looking over Trace and meeting Leni's gaze. "You don't need to be out late on Thursdays when Trace has school. Is there another day and time you'd prefer?"

"Well, my mom is already planning to help on Thursdays. She'll get Trace in bed and stay until I get home."

I consider her options. The right thing to do would be for me to move my standing weekly appointment so she doesn't have to stay out so late on a school night, but there's also a part of me that's excited to spend that little bit of time with her, even if she's working. She moves around my house so easily, even if she's just cleaning, but I really like it.

"How about this. We'll keep it as is for a bit, but if at any point it's not working for you or Trace, you let me know and we'll figure something else out, all right?"

The truth is I don't even need her to clean my place. Sure, it's helpful. I fucking hate to dust and only do it when I can write my name across my bookshelf. It's because it's her. My attraction and the fact I'm drawn to her like a moth to a flame. But I also refuse to be the reason she's missing out on things with her kid. Sure, she might need the money from this job, but she needs time with Trace more.

"That sounds good," she replies, unlocking the door. "Trace, run up and get ready for a bath."

He sticks out his bottom lip and looks like he's about to cry. "But...I want to hang out with Malcolm."

Ahhh, dammit.

My heart starts to beat a little faster as I squat down in front of the boy. "Don't be upset, Champ. I have to head home and get ready for work tomorrow, just like you have to go to bed so you can prepare for school this week." I glance up at Leni for a second before I add, "Hopefully we can still do dinner one night this week. I'll bring the fish here and cook them however you'd like. Then you can take your bath and get ready for bed."

He throws his little arms around my neck and sniffles. "Will you read me a bedtime story when you're here?" he asks, pulling back and turning those hazel eyes my way. I realize in this moment, I'd probably do anything he asked. In just a short amount of time, this little boy and his mom have wormed their way under my skin and into a place reserved solely for my family.

"You pick out the book, and I'll read it. But...you have to promise to go to sleep so you're ready for school. Deal?"

He nods and sniffles and then gives me the biggest, toothless grin I've ever seen.

I'm completely gone.

After work on Wednesday, I make sure I have everything I could need to make dinner at Leni's place. Trace told me last night on the phone he wanted to fry his fish, and when his mom came back on the phone, she told me she has an air fryer I can use. Since I've never used one, I had to do a little internet browsing at the office this morning, but it seems pretty easy and straightforward. It sure as hell beats lugging around my deep fryer, which I'd still do if that's what it took.

I'm also not embarrassed to admit I enlisted the help of my mom. She's always loved to cook, especially baking. She offered to whip up a small batch of potato salad, which goes great with fish, as well as some of her famous creamy mac and cheese. Once I told her Trace would be there, she insisted on the dish, and when she delivered it to my office an hour ago, she even had still-warm chocolate chip cookies in a container.

Alexandra Wright is simply the best.

The drive to Leni's is quick. As I approach the town square, I wave at a handful of residents out on the street. Some are window shopping in front of businesses, while others are filtering in or out of our restaurants, like Sauce It Up or the sub sandwich place. I can see kids on their bikes riding through the park, most likely on their way to the ice cream stand.

The streets seem busier now than they did midday.

I pull behind the laundromat and move to my trunk. The moment I start to unload, I hear, "Well, hello, Mr. Mayor."

I turn and find Tate standing there, as if she just left the florist. I try to keep my face void of any emotion, but I'll be honest, the last thing I need is to run into this woman when it appears I'm moving stuff into Leni's apartment.

Tate Michaels runs the *MC Scoop*, the local gossip blog, and I'm one-hundred-percent certain I now know what prime piece of intel will be featured on the front page tomorrow. Hell, probably before that. Tate has an uncanny ability of sniffing out any dirt in this town and sharing it. As the mayor, as well as a single guy who has *dated* a lot, I'm often mentioned in her little online blabbermouth page. I've come to ignore it, not even bothering to read what she writes at this point.

"Hey, Tate. How's it going?" I ask, leaving the rest of the food in the trunk.

"Good. I just stopped in and grabbed some flowers from my aunt," she says, referring to Cybill, the owner of Blossom's Florist.

"They're gorgeous. Cybill does an amazing job."

"Doesn't she?" Tate glances down, spotting the small cooler and grocery bags on the ground at my feet. "So what are you doing? Headed somewhere special?"

I give her a polite smile. "Just dropping off some food for a friend."

"Friend, huh?" she asks, her blonde hair pulled up high on her head. I can practically see the wheels spinning.

"Yep. Well, I'll let you get your blooms home," I state, grabbing the rest of my things from the trunk and closing the lid.

Just as I do, Leni comes out and opens the door. "He's freaking out in there because you haven't come up yet. Oh, hi, Tate."

The blonde woman waves and grins like she just won a prize. The gossip prize for the night. "Hi, Leni. So good to see you. Looks like you guys have plans."

Before Leni can say anything else, I head for the door, my arms loaded with bags. "Night, Tate. Have a good one," I state dismissively.

Leni holds open the door and sighs the moment it's closed behind us. "Great. That's going to be in her little blog tomorrow, isn't it." It's not a question. We both already know the answer.

"'Fraid so. Don't let it bother you, though, okay?" I instruct, leaning in and stealing a kiss from her lips before I proceed up the stairs.

Ever since I left her Sunday night with that goodnight kiss I was so looking forward to, I've thought of nothing else since. She's an addiction. One kiss wasn't enough, but it's what kept me going until today.

As I head up the stairs, I find my favorite little guy standing at the top, watching me intently. It hits me that Trace could have very well seen me kiss his mom. For the first time. When I stole kisses Sunday night, Trace was already upstairs, getting ready for his bath.

"Hey, Champ," I say hesitantly, as I step into the kitchen.

He looks at my arms and smiles. "Are those the fishes?"

"These are them, and some other stuff for dinner. How about you wash your hands and you can help me make dinner and tell me about your first day of school."

I'm rewarded with a huge grin. "Okay!" he hollers, taking off at a sprint down the hall to the bathroom.

"Did he have a good day?" I ask, setting my bags down on the counter.

"He did," Leni replies, putting the containers in the fridge. "He came out smiling and hasn't stopped talking about it since. You're probably going to regret asking him about it."

I stop and face her, setting the Ziploc baggie of fresh fish down on the counter. When she moves in front of me, I gently grab her arms and pull her into my chest. Those slender fingers grip the back of my shirt as she rests her cheek against me. "I've been waiting all day to ask him. I can't wait."

A moment later, footsteps fly down the hall and a burst of brown-haired energy emerges into the room. "I'm ready, I'm ready!"

"One more story?"

Leni chuckles, shaking her head. "You've already had one more story, and you have school tomorrow."

Trace sighs and glances up at me from the couch. "Will you read to me again soon?"

I move him so he's sitting on my lap, instead of at my side. "Listen here, Champ. Hanging out with you, whether fishing at the lake, cooking fish in the kitchen, or reading three stories at bedtime, is starting to be the best part of my day." I have to swallow over the sudden lump in my throat. "So, yes. Yes, I'll read to you again. Very soon."

Then, he throws his little arms around my neck and hugs me. "Night, night, Malcolm," he whispers, stealing my heart. I close my eyes and just soak in the moment. I never thought I'd feel like this, not toward a woman, and especially not a kid. But this kid has sunk his hook into me so deep, I'm not sure I'll ever be the same.

When he pulls away, I find myself unable to move. I watch as he hops down and reaches for his mom's hand, ready to go to bed.

Leni glances back and asks, "You okay for a few minutes while I get him in bed?"

I nod. "Take your time."

While they're out of the room, I take a few minutes to really study her home. It's definitely a small apartment, but she has all the essential space she needs for her and Trace. The kitchen is just big enough for a small round table and four chairs without being in the way. The living room houses a dark green couch with identical reclining chair, mismatched end tables, and small entertainment center with games and photos on the shelves. There's a kid-size folding table and chairs in the corner, piled with coloring books, crayons, and puzzles and a basket of other toys on the floor beside it.

It's cozy.

Homey.

I know there's two bedrooms down the hallway, a bathroom, and a closet that houses the washer and dryer, but I only know that because I saw glimpses of the rooms when I used the bathroom earlier. I know her bedroom has basic white walls, but her bedding is vibrant flowers in blues, greens, and pinks. I know she keeps three decorative pillows on the made queen-sized bed. I know she has a rocking chair in the corner of the room, probably the one she used to rock her son to sleep when he was a baby.

Maybe someday I'll get to see more of that room.

It doesn't take too long before Leni rejoins me in her living room. "Sorry about that. He had to give me extra hugs and kisses for letting you read him one extra book." Chuckling, I watch as she walks into the kitchen and opens the fridge. "Would you like a beer?"

Oh, I definitely would. One will be fine, especially if it gives me more time here. "Sure. Thanks."

Leni rejoins me on the couch and hands me the cold bottle. "I don't usually keep beer in my fridge, but my sister left a few here last week when they stopped by for a visit."

"You don't? Because of Trace?" I ask, curiously.

She opens her mouth to reply, but stops herself. After a few seconds, she finally says, "No, not because of Trace. It was actually because of Greg. He drank all the time when he was home, loved to *unwind* as he called it. I stopped buying it because I felt like I was enabling him while he was there, and I didn't want Trace to get accustomed to it, to think it's okay to drink a dozen beers every night. One or two, hell, even a few, is fine. I'm not a prude. I like to drink, but when it comes between you and your family, your obligations, then it's not worth it, you know?"

Damn, this woman slays me. Her strength and resilience are admirable, and the fact that she loves her son completely is evident. "I'm sorry you had to deal with that. It must not have been easy, single mom with no family close by."

She takes a drink of her beer. "It wasn't, but I managed. That's part of the main reason I decided to come home. I just missed everyone. Long weekend visits weren't the same. I wanted Trace to know his family."

I reach out and brush hair off her forehead before trailing my fingers down the side of her beautiful face. With my other hand, I set my drink down on the table and slip a little closer. Her breath hitches as I draw near, her tongue darting out to wet her lips. "Can I kiss you?" I whisper, my lips hovering above hers.

She meets my gaze, her hazel eyes pooling with desire. "Only if you promise not to leave me unsatisfied."

The corner of my lip turns up as a wicked smirk slowly stretches across my face. "Done, baby."

Chapter SIXTEEN

Leni

The moment his lips claim mine, heat and desire pool in my stomach and slide through my veins. I open my mouth instantly, and his tongue delves deep inside. I can feel my nipples drawing tight into little buds, a sign of just how much this man affects me.

From just a kiss.

But something tells me this isn't *just a kiss*.

Malcolm cups my jaw and crawls up onto his knees, slowly leaning me back on the couch. He never once breaks the kiss. His body presses me into the cushions in the best way possible as he maneuvers his hips between my legs. When I hitch an ankle over his ass, he rolls his hips and applies the perfect amount of pressure to the apex of my legs.

I cry out, but it's swallowed up by his mouth.

"You know, we could very easily get ourselves into some trouble here," he mutters, his lips gliding down my neck.

"What do you mean?"

"Kissing you is like a sin. A sweet, sexy, dirty sin." He nips at my flesh with his teeth. "Even though I shouldn't do it, I can't seem to stop myself."

I close my eyes and revel in the amazingness of his mouth on my skin. "Who's stopping you?" I ask, giving him complete access to my neck.

When he doesn't reply, I open my eyes and meet his intense brown stare. "Me. I shouldn't want you this badly. Not with your son just down the hall."

"He's a heavy sleeper," I reason, letting lust completely overpower logic.

Malcolm chuckles, running his hand down my side and letting it rest on my hip. With a sigh he whispers, "Oh, Lenora. You're a temptation I wasn't expecting."

It's as if he didn't mean to say that aloud.

I feel his hand everywhere as it explores my body. Yet, it never seems to land where I ache. He touches my side, stomach, and the leg hitched over his hip, but seems to avoid two key areas. The two places I'm dying for him to touch.

Just as I start to wonder if kissing is all that's on the menu tonight, he shifts his weight and runs his hand straight down from my navel to the apex of my legs. "I really, really want to touch you."

"Yes, please," I practically beg.

His eyes lock on mine as he cups me, applying just enough pressure to send bolts of pleasure through my body. Heat from his palm sears me, and I can't help but rock my hips up, needing more of this sweet torturous friction.

Malcolm adjusts his hand and slowly slips it under my shorts. I've never been more grateful for stretchy shorts in my life. His lips glide over mine as his fingers dance along the seam of my panties.

I'm just about to chastise him for drawing out the agony when he slips a finger beneath the elastic. His tongue dances with mine, a slow, seductive little number and his skin finally comes in contact with my most sensitive area. The first touch is like a jolt of electricity, hot and jarring to my overly stimulated senses.

Once he swirls his finger across my clit, he never lets up. His kisses become more insistent as he draws me closer to release. I barely have time to think, time to breathe. All I can do is feel. It's overwhelming at first but so right.

My hips are now moving entirely on their own, and it only takes a few more seconds before I'm teetering on the edge of release. Malcolm rips his lips from mine and trails them down my neck, gently biting my sensitive flesh before quickly soothing it with his tongue. The slight bite of pain partnered with his fingers is enough to send me flying over the edge.

His mouth slams into mine, swallowing my cries of ecstasy, as I ride wave after wave of pleasure. His fingers don't relent until my body sags into the couch, completely sated and boneless.

"That may have been the most amazing thing I've ever witnessed," he mutters, kissing across my jaw.

I wiggle my hand between us, seeking out his hard length wedged between us. Before I can get to him, he stops my hand, pulling it up to his lips and kissing the knuckles. "What's the matter?"

He sighs but doesn't remove my hand from his lips. "As much as I'd really love for you to touch me, I think we should wait."

His words surprise me. "Wait?"

Malcolm gives me the slightest, sexiest grin. "For when we can be completely alone. Next time, I don't want to muffle your screams, Lenora. I want them to surround me as I slide into your body for the first time. I'm not taking you on your couch with Trace in the other room. We're going on a date, just the two of us, so you tell me when you're available, but make sure you have a sitter for the whole night, because once I've got you to myself, I won't stop until we've both had our fill." He kisses my palm and adds, "And that might be a very long night."

A shiver sweeps through my body at his statement. His declaration. We've been dancing around this and both want it. I can feel just how badly he does. It's pressed very firmly between my legs. "How about Saturday night? I'll see if Laken can watch Trace for me."

He places a chaste, hard kiss on my lips. "Let me know when you talk to her. My schedule is a lot more flexible than yours."

I highly doubt that. The man works two jobs.

Then he gets up, taking the heat and comfort of his body pressed into mine with him. I didn't even realize I groaned in outrage until he chuckles and extends a hand. "What about that?" I ask coyly as I place my hand in his and he helps me up.

He glances down to where his erection is still raring to go in his jeans. "*That* will be just fine. He has a mind of his own, but it's not the first time he's had to take a seat and wait his turn," he quips with a sexy smirk.

"Well," I start, stepping up and wrapping my hands around his back, "you could always just take a long shower and pretend I'm there with you."

He groans, almost painfully. "That image is never going away now, sweetheart."

I chuckle and give him a hug. A tinge of embarrassment sweeps through me, mostly because I've never done anything like I just did with him on my couch. I've usually been in a relationship with the guys I've been...intimate with.

"If you can make it work Saturday night, we'll have dinner and then maybe head back to my place. We can watch a movie or something," he says, his own touch of nervousness in his voice.

"I'd like that." Although, my mind isn't exactly on watching a movie. There're a few other things I'd like to do with Malcolm instead...

He slides his hands into my hair and kisses me. "Thank you for letting me come over tonight and cook the fish. I had a great time."

"I did too," I reply, blushing as my mind replays what happened just a few minutes ago.

A wicked grin spreads across his sinful lips, his eyes falling to my mouth. As if reading my mind, he says, "That was definitely my favorite part." He lets me go, grabs the small bag left on the counter, and heads for the door. "Lock up behind me. I'll make sure the downstairs door is secure."

"Thank you, Malcolm. For everything. We had a great time."

His soft grin reflects in his dark eyes as he says, "Me too. Night."

And then he's gone, leaving me with the memory of the way he made my son laugh as they cooked dinner together and the way he made my body sing after Trace was put to bed. Malcolm Wright is under my skin and quickly becoming a necessary part of my day. If there was ever a chance of me keeping my distance from this man, that time has come and gone.

I just worry about the fall, because if there's one thing I'm doing, it's falling for him.

Hard and fast.

"What's the plan for this evening?" Laken asks after Trace takes off to play with the girls.

"Well, I think we're headed somewhere to eat dinner. When we talked last night, he didn't like the idea of eating at Sauce It Up because then everyone would be up in our business," I tell my sister, glancing down at my outfit.

I must have changed a dozen times. First, I felt too casual, and then too dressed up. Since I wear comfortable clothes to clean in all day, I don't have a big selection of things worthy of a date. I ended up choosing a pair of dark jean capris, a navy-blue sleeveless top that helps hide my extremely large breasts, and a pair of tan wedge sandals to give me a little more height.

"You look amazing," she says, as if reading my mind.

"Really?"

"Are you kidding? Malcolm is going to swallow his tongue when he sees you," she states with a reassuring grin.

"I'm nervous," I finally confess.

"Why?" she asks, taking a step forward and reaching for my hand.

I sigh and close my eyes. "I've seen the women he dates, Lake, and I'm definitely not one of them. Plus...well, it's been a while for me. You know..."

The smile on her face lets me know she knows exactly what I was referring to. "Listen, Leni, you have nothing to worry about. First off, let's talk about the other women he dates. Frankly, you're right. You're nothing like them."

I open my mouth to argue, but nothing comes out. At least she could have lied to me, but then again, we don't lie to each other. As sisters, we vowed to always be the one you could go to for help, and that includes hearing the hard truths in life.

"Before you get all worked up, hear my words. You're every bit as beautiful as those others, but you're real. You're not a Barbie who eats salads all day, spending her ex-husband's alimony checks," she says, referring to Jessa. "You're as real as they get. You have your own job, own two businesses, work your ass off to provide for your son, and have gotten to where you are based on your own merits, not someone else's. I'm so damn proud of you, and Malcolm Wright should thank his lucky stars you set your sights on him."

I can't help but smile.

"Now, let's talk about the *other* thing," she says, dropping her voice down to a whisper. "You've already mentioned about...*down there* when you walked in on him naked," she adds, dropping her eyes down to my groin. "Any man packing that kind of heat with the trail of broken hearts in his rearview mirror didn't get to that point without knowing how to use it."

A giggle spills from my lips, mostly because I'm recalling exactly what it felt like to have his erection pressed against me. And yes, it was...sizable.

"I've also heard the rumors and something tells me they're not too far off base."

I clear my throat and whisper, "Oh, it's not."

Her eyes widen. "How big?" I demonstrate an approximate eight-or-nine inch length with my hands, causing her to gasp. "Shut up!"

"You better be comparing the size of the fish you caught earlier in the day," Grayson states with humor in his voice as he joins us in the kitchen.

"Oh, she's definitely not talking about a fish," my evil sister retorts with a smirk. "She's talking about—"

"I'm pretty sure I know what she's talking about, babe. No need to explain. Or compare, apparently."

Laken giggles and wraps her arms around Grayson, resting her head on his chest. "Absolutely no comparison necessary. You know what I think of the size of your—"

"Stop talking!" I holler, bringing my hands up to cover my ears. "Jeez, and to think you're the quiet and shy sister."

"Oh, she's not quiet," Grayson quips, smiling like the cat that ate the canary.

"Good God, you two are gross. I do *not* want those images in my head."

"I wouldn't mind those images in my head," Grayson teases, swatting my sister on the ass.

"I'm leaving now before you two change your mind and I'm the one babysitting tonight while you go do inappropriate things to my baby sister." I start to head for the door.

"Nothing inappropriate about it, Leni! In fact, it's curl-your-toes appropriate on every level," my sister yells after me as I push through the door.

"Good night! Love you, sickos!"

"Night! I expect all the juicy details tomorrow morning."

Chapter SEVENTEEN

Malcolm

When she opens her door, it's like I'm struck by lightning. She's standing there in blue jean capris, a high-neck navy blue sleeveless shirt, and cute wedge sandals. Her hair is down and straight and her makeup subtle, yet flawless. She's simply the most stunning woman I've ever seen.

And tonight, she's all mine.

"Wow, you look amazing," I say, stepping forward and brushing a kiss across her lips.

Leni rolls her eyes dramatically, even though she smiles at the compliment. "Well, thank you."

"Ready to go?" I ask, noticing she's carrying a duffle bag too. When we talked last night, we both agreed she'd join me after dinner back at my place. There was a lot of assumptions made with no definite decisions. I don't want her to feel pressured into taking our relationship to the next level, so seeing her with a bag is a little exciting. It means she's planning on staying with me tonight.

She makes sure her door is locked and follows me to my car. I place her bag in the back seat and open the passenger door for her. Once she's inside, I move to the driver's side and hop in beside her, instantly reaching for her hand as soon as the car is started.

As I pull out, I ask, "Are you okay with a steak and seafood joint? There's this great place in Billings, and I know it's a drive, but the food is worth it."

"That sounds good. I haven't been to a restaurant that doesn't feature chicken fingers and mac and cheese in forever," she replies with a chuckle.

I automatically smile myself, recalling how much macaroni and cheese Trace put away earlier in the week when I was at their place. "Good. You'll love this joint. My grandparents and parents go a lot for special occasions. Their bacon wrapped filet is to die for."

Her stomach rumbles, causing a slight blush to tinge her cheeks. "Sorry, I haven't eaten much today."

"No? Busy day?"

She groans. "Yes. I had a cleaning job rescheduled from yesterday to today, so my mom came by the apartment and watched Trace. Then, I wasn't back five minutes when my phone rang. There was a drainage issue with one of the washing machines downstairs, which resulted in a whole drum load of water spilling all over the floor. I had to call the plumber to help, and I'm so grateful he was right next door. He had it fixed in no time."

"That's good," I reply, picking up speed as we head to Billings.

The drive takes about an hour, but it's a comfortable trip. We chat about everything, from her work and the business below her apartment to the biggest obstacles yet to come as mayor. I actually find talking to Leni easier than I've ever experienced, but to be honest, there wasn't a lot of talking on previous dates.

I didn't want to talk.

Now, all I want to do is listen to the sound of her voice as she tells me about the products she uses for cleaning.

When we arrive at the restaurant, I pull into the valet parking and lead her to the doorway. I can smell the delicious aromas as we approach the hostess stand, where a man in a suit is waiting. "Good evening, sir. Do you have a reservation?"

"We do, under Wright."

"Ahh, yes, table for two. Right this way," he says, leading us through the restaurant and toward a small, intimate table along the outer wall. "Your waiter will be with you shortly."

I hold out Leni's chair and wait for her to take a seat before sitting in the one across from her. She holds up the menu in front of her and starts browsing the dinner options. "Oh man, I'm not sure which one I want."

I don't even bother with the menu. I was here about three months ago with my dad and grandpa and already know what I'm having. It's what I always get. "Might I make a suggestion?" She meets my gaze and nods. "Go with the surf and turf. You get your option of a lobster tail or grilled shrimp skewer; both are to die for. Add the bacon to the filet. You won't be sorry."

Leni closes her menu and sets it aside. "That sounds amazing. I'll do that."

When our waiter arrives, we each order one drink and a glass of water, and I add the fried green beans for an appetizer. I find myself reaching for her hand and holding it every chance we get. Even after our drinks and the starter arrives, I constantly reach over and graze her skin with my thumb. I can't seem to stop myself.

When our entrees arrive, I smile as her face lights up and her mouth practically waters. "Holy shit, this looks amazing," she whispers the moment the waiter leaves.

"Wait until you try it."

Leni cuts into her steak and takes her first bite, "Oh my God," she groans, slowly chewing as the flavors explode in her mouth.

Only after she's swallowed her first bite do I cut into mine, savoring the amazing taste of the prime beef. "Try this," I say, digging into my lobster tail with the small fork and holding it up for her to take a bite. When her lips wrap around my fork, I almost let my own groan fly, fantasizing about her lips around something else of mine.

"Delicious," she murmurs, slipping a shrimp off her skewer and holding it up.

I lean forward, maintaining eye contact, as I bite the piece of seafood off her fork and slowly chew. The way she licks her lips as she watches me swallow has my cock jumping to full attention like a good soldier. Who knew eating dinner with her would be better than foreplay? All I can think about now is getting her home and having dessert.

We don't say much as we eat, but we don't need to. The sexual tension is so thick, I'm sure everyone around us can feel it. It's practically a living, breathing entity in the room, surrounding and encompassing us with each passing second.

Once we're finished and the waiter returns to collect our plates, he offers us dessert. When I notice her eyes lighting up as the chocolate cake is mentioned, I ask for two pieces to go and hand over my credit card. As soon as my name is scribbled on the slip of paper, I stand and reach for her hand, anxious to get her alone. Home. Naked.

All of the above.

As quickly as possible.

Leni doesn't speak as we wait for my car, one hand nestled in mine, while the other is resting on my forearm. Usually I enjoy amenities like valet parking, but all I can think about now is how I should have parked my own damn car. Then I could kiss her without being on display of others in the nearby vicinity.

Finally, my car arrives, and I practically throw the money, including a healthy tip, at the driver. Leni slips into the passenger seat, careful not to upend the bag of cake, and we're off just moments later. The first stoplight we hit, I reach for her and pull her toward me. Our lips meet in a frenzy, eager and desperate for more. Her sweet little tongue sliding against mine is almost my undoing, and the only thing that keeps me from throwing the car in park and taking her right here in the middle of the roadway is the horn blaring behind me.

I glance up, realizing the light is green, and press my foot a little too firmly on the pedal. We dart through the intersection as I try to adjust my jeans to relieve some of the discomfort. "I can't believe I almost mauled you during a red light."

She chuckles this seductive little sound that makes my dick so damn hard. "Well, in your defense, I might have been doing just as much mauling."

I shake my head as she sets her hand on my thigh. "No, I think you need to keep your hands to yourself, Lenora. If you touch me, I might not be able to control myself. You turn me into an animal," I state through gritted teeth as her fingers slide ever so closely to where my hard cock sits.

"As much as I really can't wait to see that side of you, I do suppose we should hold off just a bit until we're closer to your place. And your bed."

The groan falling from my mouth is painful. I'm so turned on it's painful. Everything is painful, except being with her.

That's pretty fucking amazing.

"You're quite the temptress, Lenora Abbott," I reply, threading my fingers with hers. "I think I'll hold your hand because I don't trust you not to do things you shouldn't do while I'm driving."

I glance over to see a wide smile spread across her lips. "Probably a good call."

By the time I pull into my driveway and straight into my garage, I'm so on edge I can barely think. I practically jump from the vehicle, not even bothering to take the keys with me. Instead, I head for the passenger door.

To Leni.

The moment she steps out, I pounce. My lips meet hers in a flurry of desire, as I press her back against the door. She goes up on her tiptoes, even in those crazy wedge shoes, and gives as good as she gets. Her hands grasp at my shirt, tugging me closer. My own hands are everywhere too. Her hair, her neck, her back, her hips. I want to touch her all over, and frankly, I'm a little overwhelmed on where to start.

Ripping my mouth from hers, I suck in a deep breath of air. "I'm not mauling you in my garage, Lenora."

"Then we should go inside, yeah?"

God, this woman is going to kill me.

Just as we practically tumble through the doorway between the garage and mudroom, her cell phone rings. Like a cold glass of water thrown over us, we both sober quickly as she digs out her device. "Shit, it's my sister's number," she says, drawing the phone to her ear. "Hello?" There's slight panic in her voice.

I step back, giving her space to take her call. Plus, the little bit of distance is probably good for me too. I'm able to breathe and try to get myself under control a little better.

"Of course it's okay. You didn't interrupt anything. Put him on."

I almost snort at her statement but hold back barely.

"Hi, buddy. I've missed you too." She listens for a few seconds before adding, "I'm glad you're having fun with the girls and Aunt Laken." She chuckles. "Yes, and Uncle Grayson too."

I walk to the back sliding glass door and look out at the water. Even though the sun has set and night has fallen, the moon is bright enough to reflect off the calm water stretching across the back of my property. I notice the solar lights around the jacuzzi are on, giving it an inviting welcome.

"Sorry about that," she says behind me, slipping her arm around my back and snuggling into my side. "Trace wanted to say goodnight. Oh, and he wanted me to make sure to tell you goodnight too."

I smile. "He's a great kid, Leni."

"He is," she agrees, gazing out over the view from my door.

"I apologize for my behavior earlier. I can't seem to help myself when you're near," I tell her, turning sideways and pulling her against my chest.

"In case you missed it, I wasn't complaining."

"Yeah, but you deserve more than to be taken against the side of a car," I reply, sheepishly. "It was probably a good thing to put the brakes on for a minute."

She looks up at me, a glint of something mischievous in her hazel eyes. "I have an idea. How about we head out to the hot tub, and you can tell me all of your reasons for needing to apply the brakes."

I groan, my dick thinking this is the best idea. "You, water, bathing suit. I'm not so sure that's a good idea. I'm barely hanging on here, Lenora," I state, reaching down while my fingers glide across the top of her ass.

"Hhmmm, you might have a point. You do seem a little…tense," she replies, flexing her hips forward and connecting with me.

"You're evil."

"Maybe," she sings, stepping back and heading through the kitchen. "Maybe not. I guess you're just going to have to put on your swim trunks and find out."

She struts away, her hips swinging and her ass so enticing in those pants. Leni heads for the garage and returns a few moments later with the cake and her bag. She places the cake on the counter and continues to move in the direction of the stairs.

Just as she starts to head up, she stops and glances over her shoulder. "I hope you don't mind if I use your bedroom to change into my suit."

Then, she disappears, leaving me with a massive erection and an even bigger desire to see what happens next.

Chapter EIGHTEEN

Leni

"You. Are. Brave. You. Are. Bold. You got this," I whisper, gazing at my reflection in the bathroom mirror. I'm wearing the only bikini I own, one I've barely worn since I purchased it years ago. It's a dark pink number with little yellow pineapples on it. The bottoms have a higher waist, which I appreciate to help cover my stretch marks and my ass, but the top leaves little to the imagination. With my girls, they practically spill out of the cups, both on the sides and in front. When you have boobs as big as mine, it's hard to find off the rack clothes that fit, especially swimsuits.

But this will work just fine.

If anything, I'm not worried about Malcolm's reaction being bad. How could it be? The man has practically been foaming at the mouth since he picked me up. Even though I still feel that familiar tinge of uncertainty, of fear. Greg used to tell me my boobs and ass were too big all the time, and after a while, it really sticks with you.

But I refuse to think about Greg and his hurtful words.

There's a gorgeous man somewhere in this house who doesn't seem to care what my body looks like naked, even though he hasn't seen it yet. The way he steals glances and constantly wants to touch me is quite telling really, so now's the time I push the worry aside.

This is me.

This is the body God gave me, and if anyone doesn't like it, well... "Fuck them," I mumble, finishing my thought.

A huge smile spreads across my lips as I give myself one last glance. "Ready or not, Malcolm Wright, here I come."

I walk out of that bathroom with my head held high. The first thing I notice is the small pile of dirty clothes tossed on the floor by his closet. They weren't there before, and upon closer inspection, I realize they're the ones he was wearing earlier. That means, he was here and changed into his trunks.

Leaving the room, I head down the hall and stairs, making my way to the sliding door. It's standing open, an invitation for me to join him. Outside, even though the air is warm, I feel my nipples pucker. From the weather or anticipation, I'm not sure, but something tells me it's more of the latter than the former.

Party lights are lit inside the small pergola. I follow the small sidewalk to the side of the structure where the opening is. I can hear the sound of the jets, as well as softly playing country music, and as soon as the hot tub comes into view, I find Malcolm sitting in the hot tub, his gorgeous chest on full display.

I stop in my tracks and watch his eyes slowly feast on my body. From head, all the way down to my knees, he drinks me in with dark, lustful eyes, causing me to shiver in anticipation.

"As much as I'm enjoying watching you stand there, you should get in. The water's perfect," he says, holding out his hand on the side to help me in.

I step onto the plastic step and into the tub, the hot water lapping at my legs. Malcolm doesn't release my hand as he guides me to the seat beside him. The water hits below my shoulders, the perfect mixture of hot and jetted. "If I had one of these, I'd be out here nonstop."

He rests his arm on the tub behind my neck. "Well, you're welcome to use it anytime you want. Especially if you're wearing that," he says, waggling his eyebrows suggestively.

"Hmm, I suppose that can be arranged. Do you come with the hot tub? I'm thinking I can get used to this," I reply boldly, turning slightly so I can run my hand across his chest. He's not overly muscular, but there's plenty of definition. He certainly takes care of his physique.

He holds completely still as I swing a leg over his and straddle his lap. I can feel his erection pressed between us, which only gives me more confidence to do this.

I spread my fingers wide across his shoulders and press my chest against his. Malcolm's large hands grip my ass, his fingers dancing along the elastic. "This bikini should be illegal in the state of Montana."

"I rarely wear it."

"Why?" his voice sounds husky and gravelly.

"Because I've never been happy with my body. I hate feeling like I'm on display, or worse that people would wish I'd cover myself up a little."

He makes a growling noise as he meets my gaze. "That's bullshit. Your body is fucking amazing. Do you know how many times I've jacked off in the shower thinking about it?"

A bubble of laughter spills from my lips. "You're nuts."

"I'm serious. From the first moment I laid eyes on you, I wanted you. You have the most erotic hourglass figure that women everywhere would die for. Your hips—"

"Are too big," I interrupt.

"Fuck that," he insists, shaking his head. "Your hips are so fucking beautiful, and this ass," he adds, squeezing it with both hands, "all I've been able to think about is watching you on all fours, this ass pointed up at me, as I make you come with my mouth and then my dick. And don't get me started on your breasts, Lenora. Yes, they may be big, but they're not my favorite feature. Do you want to know what is?"

"Not my ass or my boobs?" I ask sarcastically, even though I'm slightly uncomfortable with this conversation. I've never been a fan of feeling like I'm under the microscope.

"While those are two of my favorite features, it's not in the top spot. It's your heart," he says, catching me by complete surprise. He lifts his hand up and traces imaginary lines around the place in my chest where my heart beats wildly. "It's the way you love your son. The way you teach and nurture him. It's the way you are with your sister and your friends. It's the way your entire face lights up when you're happy, letting me catch little glimpses of the goodness that pours from it. And it's the way you make me feel when I'm around you. Like I can be me, or maybe even the person I didn't even know I wanted to be.

"So, yes, while you have amazing physical features, it's what's inside I admire the most," he states, his words raw and full of emotion.

I have to blink a few times to clear away the wetness gathering. After several long seconds of just looking into each other's eyes, I lean forward and brush my lips across his. The kiss starts slow, as if we're both savoring the moment and the feel of the other person's lips, but it quickly starts to heat up.

His hands slide down my outer thighs as I wrap my arms around his neck and hold him close. I can feel my nipples pebbling against the material of my bikini top and his erection firmly against my stomach. Even then, I need more.

He leans back and glances down at my cleavage. I pull back just enough so he can see just how hard my nipples are. Malcolm lifts a hand, hesitantly hovering his fingers at the edge of the top, as if asking for permission.

"Are we completely alone back here?"

"No one can see us. The gate's locked on the side of the house so there's no way to get back here without coming up from the water or walking through the house. We're alone."

I reach around my neck and pull on the tie, letting the two pieces fall loose. Then I grab the clasp at my back and release the closure and feel the bikini top drop into the water.

Malcolm hisses, his eyes riveted on my chest as he brings his hand up and cups the right one. He runs his thumb over the hard nub, sending shockwaves of pleasure through my body. His mouth descends, latching on to one, then the other. A groan spills from my lips as I arch my back and let him feast on my breasts.

"Hold on," he whispers, picking me up and spinning me around until I'm seated on the corner of the hot tub. "Trust me?" he asks, holding my gaze with an intensity I've never witnessed.

"Yes," I reply quickly, realizing I do. I trust him. Completely.

He smiles before dropping to his knees on the hard plastic seat inside the tub. He lifts my leg up and sets it on the side and props the other over his shoulder. Pushing my bottoms to the side, he says, "I've been dying to do this since I felt you come apart in my arms."

He lowers his mouth and...oh my.

Heaven.

As amazing as having his fingers touch me earlier in the week was, this, his mouth, is so much better. I should be embarrassed by how quickly I respond, how rapidly he drives me over the edge, but I'm not. I can't. I'm too overcome by the feel of his hot, wet tongue to care.

Malcolm grips my thighs, holding them in place, as he drives his tongue inside me before sucking hard on my clit. The action sends me soaring, flying over the edge into the glorious abyss of pleasure. I try to keep my mouth shut, still painfully aware that, while we're alone, we're still outside. And he has neighbors.

Just as I come down from the high, he pulls me into his arms and kisses me. The feel of his tongue against mine has my blood zinging once more. I wrap my arms around his neck and pull myself against him, reveling in the feel of our bare chests pressed together. My nipples are still hard and sending tingles through my veins as they slide against his body.

"As enjoyable as this relaxation in the hot tub has been, what do you say we move this party inside?" he whispers against my jaw, the bite of his stubble causing goosebumps to pebble my skin.

"I say hurry."

Suddenly, we're moving. He lifts me up, my legs wrapping around his waist and my arms tightening around his neck. I giggle as he steps out of the tub, not even bothering to dry either one of us off, and hurries to the house. His mouth claims mine as he pushes through the door, the cold air-conditioning causing me to shiver.

"No worries, love. I'll warm you up."

He makes sure the door is locked behind him before moving swiftly through the house, trailing water the entire way. Inside his bedroom, he gently lays me down on the bed, his large body covering mine.

"Is this okay?" he asks, running one hand down my arm.

"More than okay."

His mouth is everywhere. My face, my neck, my chest. Hell, even the way he kisses my shoulders is erotic and drives me crazy with lust.

When he finally pulls back, there's no denying his desire for me. It's written all over his face, embedded in his gaze, and most definitely protruding from his swim trunks. He holds my eyes as he hitches his thumbs beneath the waist of my bottoms and slowly tugs them down. They roll as they move, considering their soaking wet, and land with a wet slap somewhere on his floor.

Then, he does the same with his trunks, tugging them down and kicking them off. My legs spread as he reaches into his nightstand and retrieves protection. He has himself sheathed and covers my body in seconds.

As he lines himself up, he holds my gaze and whispers, "Ready?"

I nod, unable to find words. The anticipation is killing me, the need to feel him inside of me even greater.

When he presses inside, I gasp from the stretch and the rightness. Malcolm pauses, giving me a few seconds to adjust to his size before pushing forward a little more. He takes me in his arms and kisses me, my body completely relaxing beneath him. That's when he finally starts to move.

I can already feel my body humming, the driving need for another orgasm looming in the shadows. He rocks his hips, hitting me so deeply inside, I don't even know where he ends, and I begin.

Complete.

That's what this feels like. I'm finally complete, having found the missing piece I've been searching for in this crazy world.

Shaking off those thoughts to not get too ahead of myself, I give in to the pleasure. I cry out, his name on my lips, as I find release once more. This time, he's right there with me, chasing his own release as he pumps into me and lets go. The sight of him is glorious, the feel of his tight body stuttering and shaking, riding out our releases together is something I'll never forget. Neither is the way he instantly turns to his side, adjusting me into his body and holding me close.

"Damn," he mutters, kissing down the side of my neck as he tries to slow his breathing.

"Yeah, wow," I whisper as my fingers dance along his upper arm and wrap around his neck.

Malcolm kisses me, but this one is different. It's slow and sensual and brings all of these wild feelings to the forefront of my mind. Feelings for him, ones I can't seem to escape, even if I tried. I never pictured Malcolm as the romantic type, but he's proving to be exactly that.

"Wait here," he finally says, releasing me and rolling out of bed. "I'll be right back."

"I'm pretty sure I'm not going anywhere. My top is still floating in the hot tub," I reply with a chuckle.

Malcolm gives me a big, wolfish grin. "Good. I like having you in my bed and knowing you can't easily run away makes it even better."

He closes the bathroom door, the scent of him surrounding me. It's in his pillows and the bedding, and I find myself snuggling deeper into the bed, my eyes drawing closed.

I hear him return and feel the warmth of a washcloth as he runs it along my thighs. My eyes pop open in surprise. He throws the cloth in the hamper and crawls back into bed, shifting me and the light comforter as he goes. I'm instantly wrapped in the warmth of the blanket and his arms as he pulls me against him.

There's a sigh in complete satisfaction and contentment.

I'm pretty sure it's from me.

Malcolm kisses my forehead and whispers, "Sleep, love."

I move my hand and rest it on his chest, feeling the comforting beat of his heart below my palm. Between that and his steady breathing, it's what lulls me into a deep, peaceful sleep.

Chapter NINETEEN

Malcolm

"Good morning, beautiful," I whisper, unable to keep myself from waking her up any longer.

The first time, it was actually her who did the waking. By wrapping her mouth around my favorite appendage. Her mouth, her tongue, those lips— fucking amazing. I wouldn't let her finish me off, however, much to her dismay. Instead, I made sure she got off with me.

I've been watching her sleep for about thirty minutes, taking in every eye flutter, every time she snuggles deeper into the pillow, every sigh as she gets comfortable. I can't help but wonder how often she gets to sleep in. She's mentioned her son likes to wake up very early, which tells me, unless he's staying with her parents or sister, she's an early riser too. That's part of the reason I've let her get extra rest this morning.

But now, I just can't stop myself from touching her arm, from needing to see those gorgeous hazel eyes open once again.

"What time is it?" she mumbles, pinching her eyelids tightly together and making me chuckle.

"It's eight thirty."

"Seriously? I haven't seen this side of eight in so long, I forgot what it felt like to sleep in."

"That's why I let you sleep, but now, we have some pressing business to take care of," I tell her, shuffling myself against her side.

Leni laughs the most glorious sound. "Your business is pressing into my hip."

Damn, I love her spunk. "Not the business I was referring to, but I do like the way you think." I nuzzle into her neck and inhale her sweet scent. "I have an idea. Breakfast at Wren's, and then we can get Trace. If you don't have anything planned today, I thought you guys might like to come to the Chamber of Commerce softball game at the high school ball field. I got suckered into playing. I'm pretty sure one of the Jackson sisters had something to do with it."

She blinks a few times before giving me a small smile. "We were actually going to go to that game. Grayson's playing."

I nod. "I should have known that. I think he's on my team. I just thought Trace would like it, since he's getting into baseball. Plus, they'll have concession stands, and all the money raised goes toward the fall decorations in the park."

She sits up, holding the comforter up to her chest. "If we go, does that mean we have to cheer for you? I mean, won't everyone know...well, they'll see us. Together."

I sit up and smile. "I'm pretty sure they already know, love," I state, grabbing my phone off the nightstand and tapping on the blog post I read a bit ago. "*Is Mason Creek's most eligible bachelor officially off the market? Rumor has it a certain man in a certain political position took a certain business owner out of town for dinner and then back to his place. There have been several sightings of them together, including the one I last shared with you earlier in the week. Sounds like love is in the air once more in Mason Creek. Oh, and if she's reading this, your shoes last night were on point!"*

Setting my phone on the bed, I find Leni just shaking her head. "Doesn't that woman have anything better to do?"

"Tate Michaels? No. She has no shame. But hey, she complimented your shoes."

Her shoulders sag just a bit. "My point is only confirmed, Malcolm. Everyone, and I do mean *everyone* will assume I'm there to see you at the game."

I almost smile. "You wouldn't be?" I tease.

She blinks, catching what she said. "No, I mean, as a couple."

I take her hand from her chest, which causes the blanket to fall. No, not my original plan, but I'm not sad about it. Smirking, I finally meet her eyes. They're narrowed at me, as if I did that on purpose, but I can tell she's on the verge of laughing. "To respond to your statement, yes, I realize people would make assumptions of us being a couple, so we'll just have to put the rumors to rest once and for all."

A look crosses her face. It's part confusion, part disappointment, so I lean forward and brush my lips across hers. "We'll just have to show them that we are, in fact, a couple," I say, linking my fingers with hers.

"We are?"

"We are, as long as you want us to be."

Leni blushes and glances up beneath her lashes. "What do you want?"

"I want to date you. I want to not worry about hiding or what others will say. As long as we know where we stand, that's all that matters to me."

She smiles. "I want that too."

"Good," I reply, placing a hard kiss on her lips. "Now, let's get ready for breakfast, and then we'll go pick up Trace. I can't wait to take him to the ballpark."

"Should I ask you about your intentions?" Grayson asks, stepping up beside me in front of the dugout. I have the perfect view of where Leni and Trace sit in the bleachers with her sister, Grayson's twin daughters, and their parents, Lisa and Lewis.

"Aren't you like five years younger than me?" I quip, making him laugh.

"So. Laken suggested I do the whole big brother speech, just to make sure you don't hurt her big sister. I tried insisting I was staying out of it, while she threatened to cut me off. Since I like that particular activity with my beautiful fiancée, I thought we could get this uncomfortable conversation out of the way."

I can't help but smile. I've always liked Grayson and have gotten the opportunity to work with him often since becoming mayor. He's well liked as fire chief, thorough in his duties, and has a good rapport in the community. "Noted. I promise not to hurt your future sister-in-law, to keep you from having to beat me up after school. Deal?" I reach out my hand and wait.

Grayson laughs, shoving his hand in mine and shaking it. "Good deal. You ready to play?"

"As ready as I'll ever be. Hattie put me at shortstop because I'm quick on my feet and good with my balls," I state with a snort.

"Jesus, that's almost as bad as playing catcher because I have the best ass in town," Grayson grumbles, shaking his head.

A loud bark of laughter flies from my mouth. "And she's not in the least bit shy about her objectifying her teammates."

"Let's go, gentlemen," Hattie hollers, coming up behind us and slapping our asses. "We're in the field first."

Sighing, I head out to take my place at shortstop. I'm between Faith, who owns the salon, at second base and Brayden, the CEO of the bank, at third. When I reach my spot, I glance up to see Trace standing in the bleachers, waving at me. A smile spreads across my lips as I return the gesture, earning a big toothless grin before he sits down and dives back into his tub of popcorn.

The first half of the first inning has a couple of hits, but no runs scored. We're able to secure three outs in the first five batters, bringing us up to bat. I'm third in the line-up, so I find a bat that will hopefully work for me and take a few practice swings. While the first batter's at the plate, I hear a happy little voice off to the side of the dugout. "Malcolm!"

I turn to find Trace standing behind the fence. "Hey, Champ."

"Are you gonna bat?"

"I sure am," I state, squatting in front of where he stands. "I'm up in just a minute."

"Will you hit it out of duh park? That'd be awesome!" he proclaims, bouncing where he stands.

"I'll do my best, okay?"

"'Kay. Will you wave at me?"

Grinning, I say, "Of course I will. Why don't you run back and sit with your mom, yeah?"

He nods enthusiastically. "Bye!" he hollers, bolting back to the stands.

The crowd cheers as Tucker Simms, a local musician and mechanic, hits a line drive straight into centerfield and easily makes it to first base. I grab a helmet and head out to home plate. Spectators applaud as my name and title is announced over the PA system, so I turn and give a quick wave. I make sure to find Trace, who's standing on the bleachers with his hands in the air, who gives me a thumbs-up.

The first pitch is a little high, but the umpire, the high school baseball coach, calls it a strike anyway. The second pitch, I get a piece of it, but it bounces out of bounds just outside the third baseline. I move to the plate to wait for the next pitch, only to hear, "Go, Malcolm!" behind me.

I step back and smile at the little five-year-old in the stands, who's clearly my biggest fan today. I throw him a wave and step back up to the plate. The pitch has the perfect arch, hitting dead center of home plate when I swing. The bat cracks loudly as the ball sails high over the left fielder's head and lands in the grass.

I take off running toward first, quickly rounding the base and heading to second. I stand on the bag just as the ball is thrown in. "It's a standing double for Mayor Wright," the announcer proclaims over the cheers.

When I look across the field, I see my little buddy standing there, jumping up and down in excitement. I throw him a wave and a smile, which earns one, not only from him, but from the woman sitting just behind him and off to the left.

Jessa.

Shit.

It's a fun, close game as we finally make it through six innings of slow-pitch softball. My team ended up winning by a run, but it could have been anyone's game. When the game ends, we all meet at home plate and shake hands and take pictures. This is one of the things I've always enjoyed about my position as mayor, even if it takes forever to get through the photo part.

"Hey!" When we're finally finished and free to move about, I head straight for Leni and Trace. He runs and jumps into my arms. "Did you have fun?"

The little guy nods, his lips stained blue. "Yep!"

"What did you eat?" I ask with a laugh.

"Cotton candy. My grandpa boughted me some."

"Us too!" the twins holler at the same time, big red grins on their faces.

"Yeah, thanks, Dad," Leni grumbles goodheartedly over her shoulder to where her parents stand.

"Lewis, Lisa, good to see you again," I state, reaching out my hand and offering it to Leni's father.

He takes it quickly and replies, "You too, Malcolm. You played a great game out there."

"It was fun to do it. I hope we raised enough money for the fall decorations," I add, giving Lisa a smile.

"Oh, I'm sure you did. The concession stands had lines all afternoon," she says before turning to pick up one of Grayson's twin daughters.

As we all slowly walk toward the parking lot, Lewis says, "Why don't we all go to Sauce It Up for some pizza? Our treat."

"Dad, you don't have to do that," Laken quickly argues, but her comment falls on deaf ears.

"What else do I have to spend my money on than feeding my grandkids? You kids want pizza, don't you?" he says, his voice big and boisterous and so full of excitement. Especially because everyone knows what the kids are going to say. I'm not even a parent and I can figure it out.

"Yeah!" Trace, Harlow, and Hayden proclaim, jumping up and down with excitement.

I feel Leni wrap an arm around my waist and lean in. "Are you okay with that? I'd understand if you don't want to go."

My arm instantly goes to her shoulder. "Are you kidding? Of course I want to go along. I mean, as long as you are okay with me going."

She gives me that soft little smile I've come to love. "I'm okay with it."

"Good," I reply, bending down just enough to kiss the crown of her head.

"We're in, Dad. We'll meet you there," Leni says as Lewis and Lisa stop at the car.

"Us too. Be right behind you," Laken adds as they do the same.

As we approach my own vehicle, I notice someone standing at the driver's door wearing a painted smile.

Jessa.

Why is she waiting at my car? We never really had anything going on, just a handful of casual hookups, and there definitely isn't anything between us now. There can't be. Not when Lenora consumes my mind twenty-four seven.

My gut drops a bit as we approach, and I feel Leni's arm tense around me. She clearly sees the woman waiting, smiling some sort of fake, happy grin.

"Good game, Malcolm."

"Thanks. It was for a good cause," I state, holding on to Leni, even though I feel her try to pull away.

"I made sure to make a healthy contribution," Jessa states. Even though she's wearing big sunglasses, I can see her eyes bouncing from me to Leni.

Trace stands beside me and slips his little hand into mine. "We always appreciate the donations we receive."

She makes a purring noise in agreement and walks toward the front of my car, dragging a single finger across the silver paint, her dark red nails a stark contrast to the light paint color. "Well, I just wanted to stop by and say hello. I haven't talked to you recently, and when I saw you heading this way, I didn't want to leave without saying hello to an old friend."

An old friend.

I know her games and that comment was meant for Leni.

"Appreciate your support, but we have to get going. We have dinner plans," I state, stepping around to the back door to help Trace get into his booster seat.

"Oh, yes, I'm sure you do. One happy little family." She says the words sweetly, but I know Jessa well enough to know she doesn't mean them. She's a snooty bitch, who's used to getting her way. The fact that I'm here with Leni and Trace is clearly annoying her. It's practically written all over her Botoxed face.

"Have a nice night," I say, finally looking away to make sure Trace is secured in the seat.

I hear the click of her heels as I shut the door and turn to Leni. She's staring at me with a look of uncertainty on her face. I step forward, and place my hands on her hips. "Sorry about that."

Leni rests her hands on my chest and shrugs. "Why are you sorry? It's a public place, and you two are friends." There's something resembling worry that flashes through her eyes.

I hum, bringing her forward until our chests touch. "I wouldn't call her a friend, Leni."

Again, she shrugs. "But you know her. We both know how. She's in your past, right? We all have pasts, including me. It's nothing to dwell on or apologize for. You can't control her actions any more than you can control the weather."

I press my lips to hers. "I don't deserve you, but I sure as fuck want to keep you."

She chuckles and kisses me back with a quick peck. "Well, you're not so bad yourself."

"Let's go meet your family for pizza. They're probably wondering where we are," I say, opening up the passenger door.

"I don't know how any of the kids could still be hungry. Trace ate a pretzel with cheese, popcorn, *and* a bag of cotton candy," she replies as she slips inside my car.

"He's a growing boy, Lenora," I state, bending down so only she can hear, "like me."

Leni glances down to my crotch and shakes her head. "You're incorrigible."

Smiling, I practically run around to my side of the car and hop in, eager to go to dinner with her family.

Who would have thought?

Me.

Playboy Malcolm Wright.

Single bachelor for life.

Except that feels like forever ago.

Now, there's a new version of me.

One that has a girlfriend, who just so happens to have a son.

I seem to like him a whole lot better.

Chapter TWENTY

Leni

It's Monday morning, and my first client just so happens to be Jessa Donaldson. I've been dreading this job since I opened my calendar this morning after dropping Trace off at school. Jessa's on a bi-weekly whole house schedule, and even though I've cleaned her house since that first time Malcolm and I ran into her in the park, I'm not really looking forward to it today. There was something in her eyes last night, even though I couldn't see them directly. It was in the way she knowingly watched Malcolm and me, the way she touched his car, and the words she spoke. All I can hope is that she's lounging by her pool again today like she was two weeks ago when I was here.

As I pull into her gated driveway, I see luck isn't on my side.

Jessa's standing out front, wearing heels that probably cost more than I make in a month and a sleek jumper that appears to have fallen out of the pages of a fashion magazine, and watering her gorgeous flowers. She turns and watches me as I park behind her Mercedes SUV, not bothering to greet me as I get out of my car. Of course, my vehicle is nothing like the expensive one in front of me. Mine is several years old and is starting to rust around the left rear fender.

"Good morning, Jessa," I greet chipperly, moving to my trunk to get my totes.

"Lenora, I think we need to talk."

I stop and turn, startled to see how close she got without me hearing her move in those heels. "Sure. What's up?"

She crosses her arms over her chest, sharp, manicured fingernails tapping on her arm like an eagle talon. "I don't think this is going to work anymore."

Her statement catches me off guard. "Excuse me?" I stammer, unsure I heard her correctly.

"This. It won't work."

"Okay," I say slowly, trying to comprehend. "Why?"

She smiles, but it's not a pleasant grin. There's malice and arrogance written clearly on her beautiful face. She's not even trying to hide it. "Well, to be honest, I feel it would be awkward for us when Malcolm tires of you and comes back to me."

All I can do is blink. Repeatedly.

"Let's face it. He's not the settling down kind. Sooner or later, he's going to get tired of you roping him in to playing Daddy in your little family fantasy, and he'll realize where he belongs. With me. He always comes back to me. Always." She smiles, her perfectly straight, white teeth in a sneer.

I open my mouth to speak, but nothing comes out. As much as I want to let her have it, tell her he's not going back to her, doubt has the words dying on my lips. Because as much as I want to believe he's with me to stay, there's always that niggle of insecurity in the back of my mind, telling me I'm way beneath him. That I'll hold him back.

Malcolm has much bigger political aspirations than just being mayor of Mason Creek. He mentioned governor or senator, and let's be honest, a cleaning lady doesn't exactly make for the best arm candy.

But someone like Jessa? Beautiful, refined, and having enough money to finance whatever campaign he set his sights on? Yeah, she's a much better fit for fundraisers and television appearances.

Even if she is a raging bitch.

"Let's not make this awkward, shall we? I've written you a check for today's cleaning services," she says, holding out an envelope.

I take the payment, mostly because I really have no clue what to do. "Thank you," I mutter, shutting my trunk and heading for the driver's door.

"It's a shame this had to happen," she says, before I'm able to shut to door. "You really are exemplary at your job, Leni. It's a shame you had to stick your nose where it doesn't belong. You're a cleaning lady, a plaything in cheap shoes. It would be best if you remember that in the future."

She turns and walks away, leaving me sitting there, dumbfounded and sick to my stomach. Somehow, I get myself secured into my seat, the car started, and backed out of the driveway.

Now what?

My next job isn't until ten thirty, which leaves me with more than two hours before I need to be anywhere.

So that's what I do. I drive around, trying to comprehend what just happened and why her words bother me so much.

What a day. It turned into one of the longest I've had in a long time.

After I picked Trace up from school, he worked with me for two hours at the laundromat, selling cleaning supplies and visiting with neighbors who stopped by to chat. Once I was finished with my time downstairs, my mom stopped by to help get Trace dinner, a bath, and ready for bed, while I went back out to work.

To City Hall.

I got lucky though. As much as I wanted to see Malcolm, I'm glad he was stuck in an executive session, resulting in a longer than normal meeting. It gave me an opportunity to figure out what I was going to do in regard to losing the job this morning.

Ultimately, I decided not to mention it. Why should I? In my line of work, clients come and go. Just because this particular client was someone who used to have an *informal* relationship with the man I am currently seeing doesn't mean anything. I mean, she's probably right too. If and when my relationship status changes with Malcolm, well, she's probably saving me the heartache, because if there's one thing I know, it's the fact I'm falling fast and hard for Malcolm Wright. Knowing he was back with Jessa would hurt, but knowing he was at her house—or worse, seeing him there—would be downright excruciating.

Now, all I want to do is kick off my shoes, take a hot shower, and shake off the uncertainty I felt throughout the day. As I slip into my apartment, I find my mom standing in the kitchen, waiting. "How was work?"

"Good. How was Trace?"

She slips her purse strap over her shoulder. "Oh, he was an angel. He's such a good boy, Leni."

I can't help but smile. "He is. Thank you for always helping me with him."

Mom waves off my hand. "I'm happy to do it. I enjoy spending time with him," she says, walking toward the stairway.

"Be careful driving home," I tell her, giving her a quick hug before she descends down and secures the door behind her.

I groan in pleasure as I peel off my shoes and wiggle my toes, grateful to feel cool air on my tired feet. My next stop is down the hall to check on Trace, who's cuddled into his pillow, sleeping heavily under his favorite Spider-Man blanket.

Just as I return to the kitchen to grab a bottle of water, I hear a knock at the bottom door. Considering my mom just left a few moments ago, I worry something may be wrong with her car. I move quickly down the steps and pull open the door, only to come face-to-face with the one person I didn't expect to see.

Greg.

"Surprised?"

I open my mouth, but nothing comes out. At least not right away. Instead, all I feel is anger spreading through my veins like fire. He's standing there, smiling like it hasn't been months and months since he last saw his son.

"Well, aren't you gonna invite me in?"

What? Seriously?

"No." When he arches an eyebrow in confusion, I add, "It's late, Greg. Trace is sleeping. He has school tomorrow."

His smile falters for a fraction of a second before slipping back into place like a well-practiced response. "Kindergarten. I can't believe he's old enough," he says with a chuckle.

"Of course it would come as a shock to you. You've missed more than half of his life, Greg."

His shoulders sag as the grin finally falls completely from his face. "I know," he mumbles, averting his gaze. "I'm sorry, Leni."

Shaking my head, I reach for the door. "Don't apologize to me. I'm used to seeing your backside as you walk away, but Trace doesn't deserve this."

"I know," he says in a rush, reaching out to place his hand on the door to keep me from shutting it in his face. "Can we talk? I guess...well, I owe you an explanation. Please?"

Sighing, I step back, allowing him to enter. Even though I probably shouldn't, a bigger part is curious as to what he has to say. I'm certain I'll regret this decision, but right now, I just need to know why he kept leaving and where the hell he's been for the last eight plus months. "Be quiet," I mutter, closing the door behind him and following him up the stairs.

Greg stops in the kitchen, hand shoved in the pockets of his jeans, and glances around. "Nice place."

I shrug, stepping to the fridge and pulling out two bottles of water. Greg takes a seat and waits for me to join him.

"Thanks," he says, taking a hearty drink. "You own the place downstairs? I think I heard you used that little inheritance your grandma left you."

A smile cracks across my face as I try to figure out which of the few friends I had back in Washington shared that little detail. "Yes, I did."

He nods. "Looks like you've done good for you and Trace."

I clear my throat, trying to tamper down my annoyance. "Yes, I have."

No thanks to you.

Finally, after a few very long seconds of silence, my curiosity gets the best of me. "Where have you been, Greg? It's been months!" I demand, making sure to keep my voice down so I don't wake Trace just down the hall.

He closes his eyes, and for a second, I wonder if he's going to answer me. When he opens them and meets my fury head on, he says, "I was lost, Leni. That's the only way to describe it." He takes another deep, calming breath before he continues, "My job is all I know. It's what I do, and I love it, but when I'd come home, I'd feel restless. Even when I was with you and Trace, I just couldn't sit still. So, I'd go out. I'd meet my friends and we'd drink, but I was always moving."

Greg meets my gaze. "What I did to you, to Trace, was wrong, but I just…I guess I didn't know any different. I left you to take care of our son, and even when I was home, I wasn't present. I know that now."

All I can do is stare at him across the table. For years I waited, wanted to hear this apology, this explanation. Every time he left, and I went to bed alone, often crying because I didn't understand why I wasn't good enough. Every single time Trace asked where his daddy was and when he was coming home.

"I'm sorry, Leni," he whispers, reaching over and squeezing my shaking hand. "I was a shit boyfriend and father. You two deserved better than what you got."

I find myself blinking to clear the moisture from my eyes. So many questions filter into my head, all vying for the top of the list. It's almost overwhelming to sit here with him right now. Why is he really here? Why now? "What do you want?" I finally ask, a lump firmly wedged in my throat.

"Trace. And you."

Chapter
TWENTY-ONE

Malcolm

I'm restless as I drink my second cup of coffee. Not only did I sleep for shit, I'm still bothered by the fact I kept missing Leni last night. First, at City Hall while she was working. An extensive executive session, followed by the conclusion of the Council meeting ensured I didn't get to sneak away to my office and steal a kiss.

After I finally left the building, I shot her a quick text, only to realize she was probably already in bed. Mondays are one of her long days, with houses and businesses to clean, as well as a two-hour stint down at the laundromat.

A part of me wants to call her now, but it's still early, and on the off-chance Trace is still sleeping, I don't want to be the asshole who wakes them. Instead, I drink my second cup of joe and contemplate my next step. I still have almost three hours before I planned to be at the law office for a little work, which leaves me plenty of time to burn off this excessive energy.

After a quick change into something to run in, I lace up my favorite shoes, do a few stretches on my front lawn, and take off running. My pace is fast and hard, my heart beating just as strong. I work on controlling my breathing and feel the burn in my calves and my lungs.

I head out of town, not paying attention to the scenery around me. Usually, I enjoy the view of the mountains, of the water sources, and the trees, but today, I just focus on moving my feet, on breathing in and out, and not worrying about the fact it bothers me I haven't heard from her.

Why?

Because I've fallen for her.

Hard and fast, just like the pounding of my shoes on the roadway.

I wish I could say I didn't see it coming, but that'd be a lie. I saw it a mile away, blinking roadside lights in the middle of a dark, empty night. Like a moth to a flame, I was drawn to it.

To her.

Is this what love is? The constant need to see her, talk to her, touch her? Wanting to know how her day was and if she ate good enough during the short lunch break she awards herself? To make sure she puts her feet up and rests after taking care of everyone else? A desire to take Trace fishing all the time just so I can see the happiness on his face when he catches something?

Yeah, I think it is.

Even though I've never experienced it, I'm not dense.

I'm in love with Leni.

Probably have been since that first night I saw her standing in my office bathroom, completely stunned at finding me naked.

But do you know what? I'm not afraid of it. The man who pushed everyone aside, kept them at arm's length his entire life, finally fell. The crazy part is it was easy. She made it so damn simple just by being her.

The miles tick by as I worm my way through the backroads of Mason Creek. The sun is rising gloriously in the sky, peeking over the mountains in a breathtaking sight, and suddenly, all I want is to see her. To kiss her good morning and tell her to have a great day. I want to watch as Trace goes off to kindergarten, his Spider-Man backpack huge on his small back.

As I approach the downtown square, a few more vehicles are out and about. The coffeehouse guys, all headed to enjoy a few cups of joe and talk about the weather. I start to walk when I reach the fire station, in desperate need to start my cooldown. If I don't, I'll be a panting mess when I knock on her door.

It's just after six when I spy the back of the laundromat. I stop in the middle of the sidewalk, place my hands on my head, and take a few deep breaths. Only when I feel like my heartbeat is starting to return to normal do I continue on my way, ready to see Leni.

Movement catches my attention, and I'm instantly on alert. First, my mind prepares for trouble, only to be quickly replaced by utter confusion. The

Lacey Black

door leading to her apartment opens and a man steps out.

I stop in my tracks. He's tall, not as tall as me, but still probably around six foot. He's wearing a wrinkled T-shirt and jeans and looks as if he just rolled out of bed. He's carrying a duffle bag, and every alarm bell is going off in my brain.

He heads toward where I'm standing but hasn't noticed me yet. He pulls his phone from his pocket and curses. Just when he gets about ten feet in front of me, he glances up and startles. "Oh, shit, sorry," he says with a chuckle. "Didn't see you."

"It's okay," I reply, stepping aside as he keeps coming toward me. "Leni around?" I ask, trying to school my expression. I look to her back door before returning my gaze to the man who's now directly beside me.

"Yeah, she's upstairs. In the shower. I locked up though, so you'll have to wait for her to get out to let you in."

The hairs on the back of my neck stand on end as something foreign and unwanted races through my veins. Jealousy.

"I gotta get on the road. Have a nice one," the man says, continuing his walk to a truck parked on the side of the road. He tosses his bag across the seat and jumps in, moments later pulling away from the parking spot and disappearing.

All I can do is stand there, glancing between the vacant spot where the truck once sat and the door that leads upstairs. My mind races. Who was he, and why was he here? Most importantly, why did he look like he just spent the night? At Leni's.

My stomach churns, and I find myself walking in the direction of home. I need to think. I need a shower. I need to know who the fuck that guy was.

All I know is pounding on her door wouldn't be in my best interest. Not yet anyway. I'm aggravated and frankly, I'm not sure how to handle the energy coursing through my body. Until I can get these crazy emotions under control, I think it's best I just go home.

Maybe after a shower, I'll be able to think without feeling like I'm one step away from losing my mind.

One can hope.

When I get out of the shower and dressed in a charcoal gray suit for the law office, I finally glance at my phone. There's a message from Leni.

Leni: Hey, sorry I missed your message last night.

Me: No problem. Busy night?

It takes several minutes before she replies, and I feel like I'm about to come out of my skin.

Leni: Not really. I passed out pretty much as soon as my head hit the pillow.

I stare at her message, waiting for more. Waiting for an explanation as to why there was some guy coming out of her place at six this morning. But it never comes.

Leni: We're running late and I need to get Trace to school. Catch up later?

Me: Sure.

I wish I could say this is the point where my mind goes into a darker territory, but to be honest, it's already there. I've already thought—repeatedly—that she has done something with him. Cheated on me. And right under my fucking nose.

Even now, as I drive to the office, I can't stop picturing him walking out of her apartment. My mind, the ruthless bastard that it is, is imagining every single scenario of them being together it can come up with. And fuck, in such a short amount of time, it's come up with a lot.

I'm grumpy as I stop at Java Jitters for a cup of coffee. Not because I need the caffeine but because I need to give myself something to do with my hands, and apparently, drinking more coffee seems like the perfect fit. As I come out with my black coffee, I almost walk straight into Betsy Reed.

"Oh, Malcolm, I didn't see you there," she says, the familiar aroma of her cheap perfume tickling my nose.

"I apologize, Betsy. I was in a hurry and not paying attention," I state, smiling politely and taking a step away to continue on my journey.

"That was some meeting last night, huh?" she asks politely, oblivious to my desire to cut the conversation off and make a posthaste exit.

"It sure was. Necessary, but glad it's over." I take another step away.

"Very true. You know," she starts, following me, "I was a little concerned about you being seated as mayor."

That makes me pause. "Really?"

Betsy shrugs and pats my arm the way a grandma would her young grandchild. "I did. I knew it was in your blood, and I served with your father, my late husband with your grandfather. I was worried you were too young for such a seat."

Okay, wow. Wasn't expecting that.

"But I think you've done a lot of good for the city in your short time as mayor, Malcolm. I foresee a lot of positive changes on the horizon."

I swallow over the lump that formed in my throat. Yes, this job has been one I've wanted for as long as I was able to dream about it, but in the back of my mind, I had always wondered what everyone thought of me in that position. I won by a landslide, but I never knew if it was because of my name or the fact they truly thought I could do the job.

"Thank you. I appreciate the vote of confidence."

Betsy nods and turns to head for the coffee shop. "Oh, and it's time you settled down, young man. Make your mom a grandma, will you? She's been talking about it at church group. Maybe that nice Abbott girl, the one with the little boy you've been taking fishing and spending time with. She's lovely and would make a fine wife for you."

Then she disappears behind the glass door, leaving me standing on the sidewalk with a stunned expression on my face.

Yesterday, I would have agreed wholeheartedly. Hell, even now I agree, but I just can't get over what I saw this morning and the fact she didn't mention it. I sigh and head for my car, eager to continue about my morning. I have a client meeting at nine and another at one, and if I don't hurry, I won't have time to get settled before they arrive. Plus, my coffee's getting cold.

"You've been busy today."

I glance up and find my dad standing in the doorway to my office. "Almost finished here, and

Lacey Black

then I'm heading to City Hall for a while. There're a few things to take care of there."

Dad nods. "Well, I won't keep you."

"Hey, Dad?" I holler before he can completely disappear.

He stops and enters my office, taking a seat in one of my empty chairs. "What's up?"

"Can I ask you a question?"

"Of course." He props an ankle up on his knee and gets comfortable in the chair, waiting.

"Do you and Mom keep secrets from each other?"

If my question confuses or shocks him, he doesn't let on. "Well, I can't say on behalf of your mother, but I usually don't keep anything from her. Secrets have a way of biting you in the ass, which, as a lawyer, you're very well aware of." When I nod, he goes on. "There will always be the little things you keep, not out of malice, but out of necessity, like a surprise party or a gift, but something tells me you're not talking about those secrets."

I shake my head. "No, I'm not."

Dad sighs. "Well, all I can tell you is trust is key. You have to be completely honest with the person you're with or it won't work. Even when it's

286

something that could hurt to hear, if you don't come clean, it'll have a way of coming back around again."

"Again, with the biting of the ass," I reply with a small smile.

Dad chuckles and says, "Exactly. I made a few mistakes early in our relationship, as will you. No one is perfect, but if your relationship is going to work, you have to be willing to put in the time and effort. You have to be ready to get dirty and face the ugly that arises, and I promise you, it will. No relationship is without it."

I stop and consider his words, knowing he's absolutely right. "What if you saw something and are afraid you're overreacting?"

"Are you overreacting?" he asks, reading my thoughts.

"Maybe."

Dad snorts a laugh. "You know the first rule when sitting down with a client is to find out as much information as possible. Info is key so you can make an informed decision. Never jump to conclusions, Malcolm. Not at work and most definitely not in your personal life."

I nod, understanding what he's saying. Hell, he's not telling me anything I didn't already know, but somehow, hearing it from him, I understand a little clearer. "Thanks, Dad."

"Always, son," he says, standing up. "Oh, and bring them by soon. Your mother is dying to spend time with the boy."

"Trace." I instantly smile at the thought of him.

"Trace," Dad repeats. "We want to get to know both of them."

"I will. Promise."

He stops in the doorway and adds, "The only reason for a person to overreact is fear. Fear of losing something or someone they love, perhaps. Don't let that happen, son."

I nod in understanding before he walks out the door, leaving me alone with my thoughts. I know he's right, and I just need to talk to Leni. I'm sure there's a reasonable explanation as to who the man was and why he was there.

I just have to cool my heels until we can talk.

Chapter
TWENTY-TWO

Leni

The bell over the door announces my arrival, and I make a beeline for the front counter. "I need to talk to you."

My sister looks up from her computer monitor and smiles. "Does it have anything to do with the hunky man you spent the weekend with and brought to officially meet the family? We all decided he can stay, by the way."

I stop in my tracks, too stunned to even finish walking to where she stands. "Really?"

"Definitely. He was so good with Trace, and even Mom said she hopes things work out between you two."

I haven't had a chance to talk to either my mom or my sister since we went to dinner with them Sunday evening after the softball game, and it's nice to hear they like Malcolm.

Especially after the last boyfriend I brought home.

With reminds me of why I'm here.

"Are you okay?" Laken asks, her concerned eyes meeting my wide, frantic ones.

"No."

"Jesus, you're pale. Come sit down," my sister says, leading me over to one of the chairs meant for reading. "What's the matter?"

"Someone came by last night," I finally whisper when I'm able to find my voice.

"Who was it?"

"Greg."

My sister blinks rapidly, as if trying to comprehend what I just said. "Greg? As in *Greg* Greg?"

"Yes, *Greg* Greg. How many Gregs do I know?"

"Well, I don't know, Leni. What the hell was Greg doing at your apartment?"

I lean back against the chair and close my eyes. "He showed up last night after I got off work. I opened the door thinking Mom forgot something."

She sits beside me. When I don't continue, she asks, "What did he want?"

"He wants to see Trace again."

She sits up straight, taking a defensive stance, and demands, "Where the hell has he been these last several months? He thinks he can just show up and everything returns to like it was before? Who the hell does he think he is?"

I crack a smile at the way my little sister instantly jumps to our defense. "Believe me, I asked the same questions."

"What did he say?"

I recall the painful conversation that went deep into the night. "He apologized for not being what Trace or I needed. He said he was a selfish man and felt bad for hurting us."

"Where has he been? Why now? He hasn't seen his kid in months, Leni. Months!"

"I know, Laken. Believe me, I'm the one answering Trace's questions and seeing the disappointment in his eyes." I take a deep breath. "Greg started seeing someone a few months back."

When my sister doesn't say anything, I keep going. "She's a single mom, and when she found out he has a kid he doesn't see, doesn't even pay child support for, she broke it off with him."

"As she should."

"Her daughter's father isn't around either, and Greg saw how hard it was on Angelica; that's the girlfriend. He realized he was doing the exact same thing to me that her ex was doing to her."

"Well," my sister starts, a little calmer this time around, "karma is a bitch."

I can't help but laugh. "That it is. When he showed up, he had papers, Lake."

She sits up straight once more. "Papers? What kind of papers?"

"Child support papers. He also had a check for some of the back pay. He's going to make double payments until the rest is paid off. He also quit drinking. He realized he was on the wrong path."

Laken just stares at me with shocked eyes. "Holy shit."

"Yeah." I swallow over the emotions still in my blood from last night. "We had a good talk, really. He was the old Greg again, the one I fell in love with all those years ago."

"But you don't…"

"God, no. Not at all. Besides sharing my son with him, there are no residual feelings left for him, but as friends, we were able to come together and talk about a plan moving forward."

How could I love him when my heart belongs to someone else?

Laken smiles and squeezes my hand. "I'm glad. What's the plan?"

"Well, since Greg's job is unpredictable at times, he's going to come to Mason Creek the first weekend of the month to see Trace, starting this weekend. He'll stay at a hotel nearby, staying two nights and driving back to Washington on Sunday afternoon. When Trace gets older, we'll talk about the possibility of Trace going and staying with him a little during the summer, but I'm not ready for that yet, and Greg understood."

"Wow," my sister says, flopping back on her chair and sighing. "It sounds like the girlfriend helped him see the light."

I nod. "I think she did. They've actually gotten back together. He hopes one day to bring her and her daughter with him to meet Trace, but not yet. He needs to get to know his son first."

She meets my gaze. "And you're okay with all this?"

I think back to our long conversation, about the fear and sadness I saw in his eyes, and how emotional he got when he apologized again. "Yeah, I am. I want Trace to know his father. I wanted that all along, you know? But I wasn't going to force it either. If Greg didn't want to be in his life, then so be it."

Laken leans forward and squeezes my hand again. "I'm proud of you. I know it would have been so easy to be petty and childish, but you did what was right for Trace. So many parents focus on their own hurt and anger, wanting their ex to feel the same pain they felt, and the only one who suffers are the kids."

I nod in agreement. "Oh, believe me, I wanted to be childish and hurt him, but in the end, Trace is still the one to suffer. I told him I was worried he would flake out on us again, not showing up when he says he will, and he swore that wouldn't happen."

"Do you believe him?"

"Yeah, I do. I saw it in his eyes, Lake. If this would have been a year ago, I would have said no way, zebras don't change their stripes, but he was different this time. I saw it and felt it."

"So what now?"

"We talked until almost two in the morning. We were both exhausted from emotions and a long day. He asked if he could crash on the couch for a few hours, and while I didn't really want him to, there's no place to stay in Mason Creek. I didn't want Trace to find him there in the morning before I could have a chance to talk to him, so we agreed Greg would leave before Trace got up. He needed to get on the road back home anyway."

"That's it? He slept on the couch?"

"He did, I swear."

"I believe you, but you should probably be prepared for someone else to ask," she says.

I know instantly who she's referring to.

"Have you talked to him yet?"

"No, he sent a text message last night, but I didn't hear my phone when I was talking to Greg. And when I replied this morning, I kept it kinda vague. This isn't exactly something you talk about through text."

"No, definitely not. Face-to-face is best for something like this," she agrees.

I don't disagree, already coming to that conclusion. "Yeah," I reply. It might be an awkward conversation, telling Malcolm that Greg wants to be in Trace's life, but I think he'll ultimately be happy for my son and understand. If I know anything about Malcolm, it's that he's usually calm, reasonable, and willing to listen. They're some of the characteristics that make him an amazing, caring mayor and lawyer.

And man.

The man I love.

"Can I talk to you a bit, buddy?" I ask, tucking my son into bed after reading him a bedtime story. When he nods, I take a deep breath, recalling the phone confirmation I had with Greg just a while ago, and begin. "I talked to your dad recently."

Trace's eyes widen with excitement. "You did? Is he going to visit me?"

Instantly, I smile. "He is. He's going to come here this weekend to see you."

"Yay!" my son hollers, throwing his arms around my neck. "I've missed Daddy."

"I know you have," I reply, my throat thick with emotion. "He's missed you too. And guess what? Since Daddy doesn't live here, you can stay at a hotel with him."

He looks up at me, his face etched with confusion and worry. "But I want to stay here. With you."

"I know, sweetie, but Daddy doesn't have a bed, so he's staying at a hotel. You get to visit him there, and then come home to me when he's ready to leave."

Trace starts to cry, and my heart literally breaks wide open. "I don't want to go there. I want to stay here. With you and Daddy."

I pull him into a hug and kiss his forehead. "I'm not going anywhere, buddy, I promise. Daddy doesn't live here with us, so he's going to stay at the hotel, but if you don't want to stay there, you don't have to. You can spend time with Daddy and then come home if you want. Does that sound okay?"

He smiles through his tears. "Can Daddy stay here too?"

"Oh, well, I don't know about that, buddy. We'll see." I reach down and wipe away his tears. "I love you, Trace."

"Love you too, Mommy," he whispers, snuggling back into his bedding and curling onto his side. I push hair off his forehead, place a kiss on his soft skin, and slip off his bed and out of his room.

When I reach the kitchen, I instantly grab the last bottle of beer, wishing I had something stronger, even though what I really need is a hug and a bed, preferably both with Malcolm. I pop open the top and retrieve my phone, anxious to contact the man I can't stop thinking about.

Me: Hey. It's been a crazy, long day. You around?

I set my phone down on the counter and start to fill the sink to wash the dishes from dinner. I also make a mental note to text Greg about my conversation with Trace, so he's prepared to possibly bring his son back here Friday and Saturday night. If Trace doesn't want to stay with him at a hotel, I won't force him.

By the time I finish washing tonight's dishes, I glance over at my phone and find the screen blank. I tap the text message app, just to make sure I didn't miss the notification, only to confirm he hasn't responded. I finish off the beer, wondering if he's stuck at City Hall or something else came up, but deep in my stomach, it's like a pit of dread and misery.

After making sure the door is locked, I return to my apartment, wash my face and brush my teeth, and climb into bed. It's still early, but after only getting a handful of hours of sleep early this morning, I'm too exhausted to stay up much later.

With my phone curled in my hand, I close my eyes and slowly drift off to sleep, thoughts of Malcolm and his reckless grin accompanying me.

My phone chimes, waking me from a heavy sleep. It takes me a few seconds to get my bearings, but when I do, I glance down at my phone. It's still clutched in my hand, so I tap on the screen to bring it to life. I have a message, but it's not from the person I had hoped.

Laken: You awake?

Me: I am now. What's up?

Laken: Have you talked to Malcolm? Tell me you talked to him, Leni!!!!!!

Me: Damn, why so many exclamation points? I sent him a message last night to talk, but he didn't reply.

Laken: OMG OMG OMG!

Me: What? You're kinda freaking me out.

I glance at the clock and notice it's five thirty.

Laken: Ok, so I couldn't sleep this morning and got up. I went online and was browsing social media when I saw a new blog post on the *MC Scoop*.

I groan aloud and switch screens, pulling up the internet. I go to the site my sister was referring to and find a blog entry dated for late last night. When I click on it, my heart drops into my stomach, my lungs refusing to move oxygen.

Well, I do admit I was a little shocked tonight by what happened at Pony Up. The place was pretty empty, but that didn't stop a certain man in the top political position to share a drink with a much older widow/divorcee he's been known to hang out with from time to time. Not shocking their drinks lasted until way late. What was shocking was the fact they left together and were not very discreet about it. All I can hope is that the relationship status of the other woman he spent last weekend with is done and over with, because if not, someone has some explaining to do.

I sit, completely stunned, and stare down at my screen. I reread and then reread again, only to find the post exactly as it was the first time around.

My phone continues to chime in my hand, so I quickly switch over to text.

Laken: WTF?!

Laken: Are you there? Did you read it?

Laken: Leni? My God, I'm so sorry! What a fucking asshole!!!!

Me: Wow, OK. Wasn't expecting that.

My heart hammers so hard in my chest, I'm terrified it'll wake up Trace.

Laken: I'm so sorry, Leni. So damn sorry.

Me: It's OK. Not your fault. Listen, I gotta go, K?

Laken: I feel terrible, but I couldn't let you not know. Besides, it's the *MC Scoop*. It might not even be true anyway! You know how rumors are in this town.

Me: You're probably right. They're terrible.

Laken: Sorry to wake you with this, Len. I hope it's not true. Love you.

Me: Me too. Love you more.

I set my phone down just as the device indicates I have a low battery. I don't even bother plugging it in. My mind is racing, my heart hammering and maybe even breaking a little in my chest. All I can think about is Jessa on Monday, firing me because she knew he'd come back to her. Was it a complete coincidence they had drinks last night or was she warning me it was coming much sooner than I anticipated?

Perfect Kiss

Either way, the pain in my chest is excruciating. It consumes me with the agony of a thousand knives stabbing through my skin.

I jump out of bed and head for the shower. There's no way sleep will return anytime soon. As I lather my hair, I tell myself not to get too far ahead of myself. I'm sure this could all be easily explained. It's the *MC Scoop*. Half of the posts are exaggerated or made up, right?

Right.

Then why does it feel like someone just cut out my heart with a dull butterknife?

TWENTY-THREE

Malcolm

My head is pounding. So. Fucking. Loud.

I open my eyes, but the thumping continues. It takes me a few seconds to realize it's not coming from my head, but from the door.

I jump up, thankful to be wearing at least a pair of shorts, and stumble out of my bedroom. My legs are slow to keep up, thanks to the extensive workout I endured late last night, and then again early this morning.

Just as I hit the stairs to go down, I find a figure standing there, hands on her hips and tapping her foot on the hardwood. I feel like a scolded child all over again. "Took you long enough to answer the door. I ended up letting myself in."

"I see that," I mumble, walking down the stairs, past my mom, and straight to the kitchen for coffee. The timer was automatically set, so I grab two cups from the cabinet. "Want some?"

"Please," Mom says, taking a seat at the table and waiting on me to join her.

"So, what do I owe this early morning visit?" I ask, setting her cup in front of her and grabbing the sugar.

"Early?" she asks, arching a perfectly manicured eyebrow heavenward.

I glance at the clock on the oven and wince. When was the last time I slept until almost eight o'clock? On a Wednesday? Never. "I had a late night, and since no client appointments until later, I decided to take it easy this morning."

She sips her coffee delicately, but never averts her gaze from mine. I feel like a high schooler again, about to be interrogated by the great Alexandra Wright for something she probably already knows I did. She continues to just watch me, waiting.

"Why don't you save us both the time and just tell me what I owe this spontaneous visit for?"

She grins. "Am I not welcome to drop by and say hello to my favorite son?"

"Your only son," I start, taking a healthy sip of coffee and scalding my tongue, and grabbing a seat. "Considering you rarely stop by unannounced, I figured there was a reason."

"Oh, there is."

I glance up and meet her gaze, not liking the intensity and scrutiny reflecting back at me. "Well, let me have it," I state, sitting up straight and preparing to take my licks.

After the world's longest ten seconds, she finally asks, "Are you hungover?"

Her question surprises me. "No. Why?"

"Well, considering you were at the bar last night and were still sleeping at eight, I figured you tied one on last night."

My eyebrows shoot up in confusion. "I went for a run late last night, and then again this morning at about three when I couldn't sleep." Her look is laced with skepticism. "How did you know I was at the bar?"

"You mean how did I know you were there and left with a certain woman who was *not* Lenora Abbott?"

I sit up straight and narrow my eyes. "How do you know that?" I ask, my mind racing. There were only a few others in the bar last night, some regulars, but they didn't appear at all concerned with me or the woman who showed up looking for someone to buy her a drink.

"The question shouldn't be how I know, but what did you do? I don't need details. I'm still your mother, but I'm sure I'm not the only one who'd like to know why you were with that dreadful woman. I'd know she'd love nothing more than to sink her teeth into her next cash cow, but I had really hoped it wouldn't be you."

I shake my head, trying to process what she's saying. "I was already there when Jessa showed up. I bought her one drink, but she was hitting it pretty hard. I escorted her outside to get some fresh air and then gave her a ride home. She was in no condition to drive." I leave out the part where she threw herself at me the moment we arrived at her house, trying to get me to come inside.

Mom sighs. "Listen, Malcolm, you know how this town is. Nothing is private. I don't know who saw you leave with her, but it's all everyone is talking about."

I close my eyes as dread fills my gut. I really was trying to be a good guy and help her home. Nothing happened. At least nothing more than her kissing me and grabbing at my dick, both of which I shut down right away.

The truth was, as much as I felt hurt by what I saw at Leni's apartment, I couldn't do anything with Jessa. How could I when I was consumed with a gorgeous brunette with big hazel eyes and a laugh that makes my heart so fucking happy, I can't even see straight.

"Jesus," I mumble, knowing what this means. "I'm sure Leni has already heard too."

Mom sips her coffee. "I'd be surprised if she hasn't."

I jump up and go in search of my cell phone. Where the hell is it? I didn't even notice I didn't have it on me when I went for my runs, just wanting out of the house and to feel my feet pounding the pavement. When I run upstairs and check my pocket, only to come up empty, I return back to where I left Mom. "I don't know where my phone is."

"Listen, Malcolm, I don't know what's going on, but if you need to talk, I'm always here."

"Thanks, Mom, but I really just want to find Leni right now, okay?"

She nods and goes to dump her cup of coffee down the drain. "I pray you find her and can work this out."

I meet her gaze. "This is bad, isn't it?" I really don't need her to confirm what I already know.

"It'll be okay. Just talk to her and tell her how you feel."

Panic sets in. How I feel? Do I even know how I feel?

Yes. The answer is a resounding yes.

I've fallen in love with her, but when I finally say those words, it won't be to my mom.

Mom gives me a knowing smile and heads my way, kissing me on the cheek. "Go find her and explain. I'm sure she'll hear you out, but if not, that's okay too. Give her a little time to think, but not too much time, okay? Be respectful and understanding, not overbearing and demanding like you were as a child."

I can't help but snort out a laugh. "Understood."

She places her hand on my cheek and smiles softly. "It might not be easy, but anything worth keeping rarely is. Go get the girl, son."

I take off up the stairs, determined to get ready so I can find Leni. As much as I'd love to just run out the door now, I don't think me searching town in just shorts is the way to go about it. Even though I showered after my second run early this morning, I take another one. If anything, the cooler water helps wake me up and strengthen my resolve.

As I dress in a pair of khaki pants and polo shirt, I think back over last night. How I wanted to drown my sorrows in alcohol, but only being able to get two drinks down. How Jessa showed up looking like she just returned from the salon or the plastic surgeon or possibly both, asking me to buy her a drink. I did, out of sheer politeness, and maybe because I didn't really want to be alone. I think back to the time we spent at the bar, only to realize now I don't think she drank as much as she led me to believe. I recall the single drink I bought her, as well as one more from a regular down the bar. It wasn't nearly enough to get her so intoxicated she couldn't walk without stumbling. I was so damn preoccupied with thoughts of Leni and how I wanted to talk to her, I didn't even notice what was right in front of me.

Jessa played me.

And now everything is fucked up.

Royally.

I spend all morning looking for her, to no avail. Without having my phone, I can't call her, so I'm left with driving around. It's Wednesday morning, so she should be working, but I can't seem to find her car at any of the places I'd expect it to be.

Out of desperation, I pull up in front of her sister's bookstore, One More Chapter, and get ready to face the firing squad, because if there's one thing I know, if Leni is aware of the rumors about me and Jessa, her sister is too.

I step out of my car, shove my keys into my pocket, and head for the door. A bell announces my arrival. The moment my eyes adjust to the dimmer light, I find the woman I'm looking for behind the counter, glaring daggers.

Yep, she's heard.

"Hey, Laken," I say, slowly taking a few steps in her direction.

"What are you doing here?" she asks, averting her attention down to the stack of books on the counter.

"I'm looking for your sister," I announce, deciding to not beat around the bush.

"I have no clue where she is." Again, she refuses to look up, a sign she probably knows much more than she's letting on.

I sigh and stand politely in front of her. "Listen, Laken," I start, but am interrupted.

"Don't you *listen, Laken* me! You have no right coming in here and asking for her. Even if I did know—which I don't—you'd be the last person I'd tell after what you did."

"I know this looks bad, but you have to believe me, I didn't leave with Jessa. Not the way it looks," I insist.

Laken rolls her eyes in a way that reminds me of her older sister. She turns and grabs another stack of books and practically slams them down on the counter, a sure sign of her agitation. "I'm probably not the one you should be telling this to."

"No, I agree, but I haven't been able to find Leni. I've driven everywhere in this town and can't find her car. I lost my phone somewhere, so I can't call or text her. I just want to talk to her, to explain."

She finally meets my gaze. "I think you've done enough," she whispers, her voice hoarse with emotions. It kills me because if she's this upset, that means her sister is too. The thought of her off somewhere, crying, is like a knife blade to the sternum, and at this point, I think it might be welcome.

"That's where you're wrong," I insist. "I won't stop trying to find her, Laken. I need to explain what happened. It's not how it looked, honestly. Yes, we were at the same place at the same time, and yes, I left with her to drive her home because she had been drinking, but I went home alone. I swear."

The hardness in her eyes starts to ease a bit as she considers my words. I only hope she's willing to help me out now that she knows I wasn't off screwing Jessa. "Listen, I get how the gossip can run wild in this small town, but I really don't know where she is. I haven't talked to her since early this morning, okay? She was upset, as anyone would be. I texted her a bit ago, but she hasn't answered yet."

I sigh, wishing I was closer to finding her. "Okay. Will you do something for me, please? If she gets back to you, will you tell her I'm looking for her? I really need to speak to her, Laken. I just...I have to explain." I close my eyes, dread filling my gut. "This can't be the end. Not like this."

When I open my eyes, she's watching me. "I'll tell her."

I nod in appreciation. If there's one thing I've learned in the last handful of hours, it's that there's an explanation for everything. If the rumor mills have it wrong about me and Jessa, then I damn well could have it wrong about Leni and the mystery man from her apartment. When I think back to our time together, never did I think she was someone I couldn't trust. If anything, it's the exact opposite. I trust her more than I've ever trusted another human being in my life, outside of my immediate family.

That thought is startlingly soothing.

"Thank you," I state and move to the door.

The sun shines brightly in the late morning sky, despite my mood. A quick glance at my watch confirms I need to go to the office. Despite preferring to continue my search for Leni, I know I'm at the end of the line. All I can do now is go to work, try to get a little done, and maybe get my mind off everything that's transpired in the last two days. Laken said she'd give her sister the message to get ahold of me if and when she talked to her, so now all I do is wait.

It's like the universe knows I'm terrible at that.

I need to find my damn phone.

Chapter TWENTY-FOUR

Leni

What a day. I'm exhausted, emotional, and ready to crawl into bed, and it's only seven.

When Trace got out of school, I picked him up and went for a ride. I didn't have any other scheduled clients today, so we got on the road and drove to Billings for dinner. We found a great hamburger joint, placed an order to go, and took our meal to the park, where he played until he was practically ready to pass out himself from the fun. Now, we're back home, and all I can think about is bedtime and maybe a bottle of wine.

The first thing I do when I unload my bag on the counter is plug in my phone. It's been dead all day, but it hasn't bothered me. In fact, I've enjoyed the break. It was nice to shut everything off and just be.

Do I feel guilty? Sure do. I own a business, and even though my dad's number is listed as a secondary emergency contact for the laundromat, I still should have charged my phone before now. The thing is, I knew what would happen if I had a working phone. I'd reread that blog post and obsessively scour the internet for more. Social media wouldn't be my friend, that's for sure. So I did the one thing I'd probably chastise someone I loved for if the shoes were on the other foot and kept my phone off.

As soon as it gets a little juice, I see it power on, and I dread what I'll find when it's back online. Instead of waiting, I head down the hallway toward the bathroom and start the tub. "Hey, Trace, get ready for your bath. The tub is filling up," I holler, setting a clean washcloth onto the side of the tub before I head across the hall.

"Can my friend Parker come over this weekend?" he asks, stripping his shirt and shorts off and throwing them in the hamper beside his closet.

Trace has been talking about Parker Carlson since he got into my car after school. Parker is the son of one of my clients, the local physician, and they've been playing together at recess. "Not this weekend. Daddy's coming for a visit, remember?"

"Oh yeah!" he says, a hint of excitement in his hazel eyes. "But I don't have to stay at the hotel, right?"

"Not if you don't want to. Daddy and I will figure it out when he gets here Friday, okay?"

Trace nods before running across the hall, stripping off his underwear, and jumping into the tub. "Can I have my boat?" he asks, pointing to the plastic toy I keep outside of the tub. Otherwise, it's so large, it falls into the tub and I trip over it while I'm showering.

"Keep the water inside the tub, will ya? I'll be back in a few minutes," I announce, shutting off the tap and returning to the kitchen to check my phone.

Of course, it blew up. I have fourteen missed calls and twice as many messages. Guilt consumes me even more as I scan the names of the missed calls, knowing they'll be the same names in my text messages too.

Laken: Just checking on you.

Laken: I'm sure you're busy working, but still wanted to see how you're doing. I know today has sucked. Let me know.

Mom: Hi, sweetie. Laken just called here looking for you. Is everything ok?

Laken: I called Mom. Don't make me call Dad too.

Laken: This isn't funny. You better be super busy or stuck in the bathroom with explosive diarrhea. Those are the only excuses for not texting me back.

Laken: This isn't funny. I'm getting really worried.

Laken: Grayson is on his way to your apartment.

Laken: You're not there. Where are you?

Laken: You better be dead! No, I don't mean that. I'm just really worried, Len. Call me. NOW!

Fuck. This is bad.

I press the call button and bring the device to my ear. Laken answers on the first ring. "What the absolute fuckity fuck, Leni! I've been terrified someone kidnapped and murdered you!" she bellows.

"I'm so sorry, Lake. My phone died this morning, and I didn't charge it. I didn't mean to scare you," I reply, feeling like a small child, full of embarrassment and regret.

"It's not just me. Half the town's freaking out."

That makes me pause. "Half the town?"

She sighs. "Well, no, not half the town. But Mom and Dad have been calling you, I made poor Grayson go looking for you while I was at work, Justine has been keeping her eye out, and then there's Malcolm," she says, pausing after she says his name. "You should call him."

Now it's my turn to take a deep breath. "I'm not sure that's a good idea right now."

"No, it's absolutely the right idea. Call him, Leni. He's beside himself. He's been looking for you all day."

"Where at? Pony Up? Jessa's house?" I retort, unable to hide my hurt.

"Listen, Len, this isn't my story to tell, but just know, sometimes things aren't what they seem. This town has a way of getting it wrong and making it worse with each repeat. You of all people should know that."

I close my eyes, the words from the blog coming back to me. How could I have gotten it wrong? Either they left together or they didn't, right? "I'm sorry I upset and worried you. That was never my intention. I forget sometimes what it's like to have a tribe in your corner."

"We were always in your corner, big sister, but from a much farther distance. Now that you're back in Mason Creek, we're right beside you."

"I know, and I appreciate that more than you'll ever know. I hate to ask, but can you call Mom for me. Apologize and tell her about my phone. Tell her Trace and I went to Billings for dinner and are home now. I promise to call her tomorrow."

"Yeah, I'll call her as long as you promise me something."

"What?"

"You'll let Malcolm know you're okay."

"Lake," I grumble, throwing a slight temper tantrum like a spoiled child.

"Please, Len. If you don't, I will. He's been worried sick."

I take a deep breath and concede. "Fine, I'll send him a text message before I help Trace wash up in the tub."

She sighs in relief. "Thank you. And yes, I'll take care of Mom."

"You're the best," I say, meaning it with my whole heart.

"Naw, you'd do the same for me. Now go. Give my nephew a kiss from me."

"Will do," I say before signing off.

Knowing I need a few minutes to collect my thoughts before I send the text she's pushing for, I check on Trace in the bathtub. He's wearing a huge toothless grin and covered in soapy bubbles, having grabbed his shower gel and scrubbing himself from head to toe.

I help him finish his bath, and the moment he's wrapped in a towel, he holds up his hand and says, "Look! I'm all pruney!" and bursts into fits of giggles.

"You are, pruney boy. Go put your underwear and pajamas on, and I'll get a movie started in the living room."

"Can we watch the baseball movie?" he asks, excitement filling his eyes.

"Yes, we can watch *The Sandlot*, but we won't be able to see the whole movie tonight. It's a school night, and you have a bedtime."

"Okay. But can I see to the part where the big dog chases them?" His eyes are full of excitement.

"Probably not, buddy. That's toward the end of the movie. We'll watch for thirty minutes, and then we'll read one book. Sound like a deal?"

He nods before taking off into his room to get into his pajamas. As I fire up the DVD player and get the movie set, there's a knock on the door downstairs. I don't have a lot of visitors here, but occasionally someone using the laundromat has a problem they need help with, so I hurry downstairs to see what the problem is. When I glance through the peephole, a gasp falls from my lips.

My hands are slightly shaky as I turn the lock and open the door. Our eyes meet, and I swear I feel waves of relief rolling off his body. The tightness in his shoulders just seems to fade away, and the faintest smile plays on his lips. "Thank Christ," Malcolm mutters, closing his eyes for the briefest second before finding my gaze once more.

"What are you doing here?" I ask, my voice small and tight. Damn, he looks good, even if his clothes are slightly wrinkled, his hair a little wild, and he clearly didn't shave this morning.

"I've been looking for you," he states, as if that's the most logical answer in the world.

"I'm sorry. My phone died this morning, and I didn't have time to charge it," I answer, even though that's not entirely true. I could have found time, just didn't want to talk to anyone.

He nods once and holds my gaze. After a few long seconds, he finally asks, "Can I come in? And talk?"

I glance up the stairs. "Trace is getting ready to watch a movie, and—"

"Please, Leni," he whispers, his eyes full of pain. "We can wait until he goes to bed, but I really think we need to talk. There's some things I need to explain, and then if you want me to leave, I will."

A huge part of me wants to shut the door, to push him away so this horrible hurt in my chest will dissipate, but I know he's right. That's why I take a step back and hold the door open for him to enter.

"Thank you," he says, brushing past me as he steps inside the small space. My body instantly responds to his nearness, his touch, his scent. It's like it doesn't care he betrayed me. One graze of his skin against mine sets me on fire with desire, despite the overwhelming disappointment and anger I feel.

Go figure.

I lock the door and head up the stairs when he doesn't move, waiting on me to ascend first. Just as we step inside the kitchen, Trace bursts from his bedroom. "I'm ready to watch…Malcolm!" he exclaims, changing the course of his statement and the direction he's running. My son runs straight to Malcolm and throws himself in his arms.

"Hey, Champ," Malcolm replies, catching him easily in his arms and returning the hug my little boy gives him.

"Did you come to watch *The Sandlot* with me?" Trace asks, eyes wide with anticipation.

Malcolm looks at me for direction. I don't want to talk with little ears within earshot, so I nod. "Sure, I can watch a little bit of it with you," Malcolm responds, setting Trace down on the worn linoleum.

Trace takes his hand and drags him into the living room. They sit together on the couch, my son tucked comfortably into Malcolm's side, as I press the play button on the remote. The entire time, I try not to look over at the picture-perfect image they create.

The movie starts, and I take the opportunity to wash a few dishes in the sink, making sure to keep my eye on the clock, since it's already approaching bedtime. Every time Trace says something to Malcolm or gets excited at one of his many favorite parts of the movie, I can't help but feel a tinge of sadness. What if this is the end? Trace will be losing someone he has quickly become accustomed to having in his life. A friend. Someone who takes him fishing, includes him in our date nights, and is currently making promises to play catch with him very soon.

It hurts too much to think about having to explain to Trace why Malcolm isn't coming around anymore.

I close my eyes and hang my head, trying not to think about the hurt my son will feel. It's the same hurt I saw in his eyes every time he asked about his dad and I had to tell him he was away working. Greg better not flake out on him again. If he loses Malcolm, and then Greg too, I'm not sure Trace's little heart can stand it.

Warm hands are hesitantly placed on my shoulders before gently squeezing in support. "It's going to be okay, Leni. I promise," Malcolm whispers, kissing the back of my head and holding me close.

He leaves me torn between wanting him to throw his arms around me and hug me tight or to not touch me because it hurts my heart too much. The former is currently outweighing the latter at this moment.

When the clock finally hits thirty minutes, I turn off the DVD and remind Trace of his bedtime. Instead of grumbling and begging for more time, he turns to Malcolm and says, "Can you come over tomorrow and watchded the rest of the movie with me?"

Malcolm grins. "We'll see, Champ," he says, giving my son a warm, positive smile that doesn't quite reach his eyes.

"Okay," Trace says, throwing his arms around Malcolm's neck. "I love you."

Tears burn my eyes as I watch the display. Malcolm closes his eyes and smiles. "I love you too,

Champ." It literally feels like my heart is going to burst from my chest.

Trace jumps down and heads to his bedroom, most likely to pick out the book I'm reading tonight. "I'll be back," I whisper, my voice hoarse. I don't wait for Malcolm to reply. I can't. I hightail it from the room, finally able to take a deep breath when I crawl onto Trace's bed.

"This one," he says, handing over the fishing book he picked out from my sister's store.

I open the book and start to read, knowing this book will always remind me of the man in my living room. The one who stole my heart and may be about to give it back in pieces.

Chapter
TWENTY-FIVE

Malcolm

Curiosity gets the better of me. I slowly walk down the hallway, entranced by the sound of her voice as she reads. I lean against the wall and close my eyes, letting the sweetness of her words wash over me. When she gets to the end, she tells him how much she loves him and wishes him goodnight. His tired little voice says the same, and I can picture her tucking his Spider-Man blanket under his sides like she did the last time I was here.

Instead of retreating to the living room, I stay there and watch as she exits her son's room. Our eyes meet, but instead of the brightness, the happiness I'm accustomed to, they're filled with a sorrow that feels like an arrow straight to my chest.

Silently, we walk to the kitchen. I take a seat at the table, even though I'd prefer the comfort of the couch. Something tells me she'd feel more comfortable with the round hard surface between us.

For now.

"Would you like something to drink?" she asks, possibly trying to distract herself for a few more minutes.

"No thank you."

Leni grabs a bottle of water and finally joins me at the table with a sigh. I wait until she finishes fidgeting and takes a drink of her water before I begin.

"I owe you an explanation and an apology, but not for the reason you think."

"Why do I think you're apologizing?" she asks, her voice laced with challenge.

"Because you read the blog gossip and think I did something with Jessa." When she doesn't reply, I go on. "Not that I'd blame you," I quickly add, "But that's not what happened."

"What did happen?"

I sigh. "I went to Pony Up after I left City Hall. I wasn't even halfway through my first drink when she walked in. There weren't many people there, a handful of regulars, so she came and sat next to me and asked if I was buying her a drink. I did, being polite, and we chatted for a bit.

"When she had her second drink, I wasn't the one to buy it. One of the guys at the end of the bar did, and she thanked him by ordering a round of shots. I had just finished nursing my first and only drink, so even with the shot of whiskey, I wasn't anywhere near drunk. In fact, I felt completely fine.

"When I was ready to leave, she appeared pretty tipsy, stumbling around a bit on her heels. I didn't feel comfortable letting her drive home like that, so I offered to take her. We walked out of that bar together, but it wasn't because I was going to sleep with her. I swear."

Leni nods and looks down at her bottle of water.

"When I took her home, she tried to kiss me." Now her eyes are back on mine. "I pulled away quickly and told her I wasn't interested. She tried to get me to come inside, but that wasn't happening. There was no way I was going to jeopardize what I have with you, not when I finally found something worth hanging on to."

She swallows hard, her eyes filling with tears. It has me moving, switching to the chair closest to where she sits and taking her hand in mine.

"I shouldn't even have been in there. I should have come straight here when I had questions about what I saw here yesterday morning, instead of arguing with myself and making assumptions."

Leni sits up straight. "What you saw?"

Now it's my turn to avert my gaze and exhale loudly. "Yeah. I went for a run yesterday morning and was going to stop by and steal a kiss. When I was walking toward your door, a man was just leaving. He had a bag with him, and my mind went to the worst place possible. I should have called and talked to you, but I didn't. I assumed the worst, just like I'm sure you did when you saw that post."

A single tear falls down her cheek, simultaneously ripping my guts out of my body. I hate seeing her cry, especially when I'm the cause. "That was Greg," she whispers, sniffling and wiping her nose with a napkin. "He stopped by unannounced Monday night. I was already having a terrible day, and then I opened the door and found him standing there."

My heart kicks up a few extra beats on hearing the name of the man I saw. I'm not sure if I should be happy or upset by that news. I adjust my position on the chair so her legs are between mine and hold her hand on my knee. "We're going to get into why you were having a bad day, but first, what did he want?"

"So much," she says, and then tells me all about him realizing he was being a shitty father and how he saw the light when he met his current girlfriend. I listen as she explained why he was still there in the morning, understanding her side of the situation and why she allowed him to stay.

"He's coming here this weekend then?" I ask, brushing my thumb over the top of her knuckles and watching as a shiver sweeps through her body.

"He is. He should get here around six on Friday. He already has a hotel room, but Trace is adamant he's not staying with him there. He very well may change his mind by the time Greg is here, and that's okay. Either way, I just want him to get to know his son and be a part of his life, but only if that's what Trace wants. I won't let him come in and out whenever the mood strikes him."

I bring her hand to my lips and place a kiss on the very knuckles I was rubbing. "You're an amazing mother, Lenora Abbott."

"I try, but some days are harder than others."

Meeting her gaze, I say, "I'm so sorry. I shouldn't have made assumptions and should have talked to you immediately, and I definitely shouldn't have gone to the bar when I was upset. This whole thing could have been avoided if I had just called you."

"I'm sorry I believed the chatter in the blog instead of talking to you too. I think we both messed up," she says, leaning into my arms as I pull her close.

My body starts to calm for the first time since yesterday morning when I wrap my arms around her shoulders and breathe in her familiar scent. I'm at peace, her head resting against my chest and her arms around my waist. Even though we're both still sitting, it feels so natural and right.

"I wish I knew how the *MC Scoop* caught wind of me and Jessa leaving the bar together," I say, almost absently. It's something that's still bothering me since I read the post. "There was no one around."

Leni pulls back and gazes up. "Tate has a way of hearing and seeing everything."

"True," I concede, yet something doesn't add up. "I just don't see the old guys in there running and telling her about it, ya know?"

"Who knows. You are a pretty hot commodity around here," she teases, giving me a coy grin.

"This is true, but still. Just funny the only people around were us and two old guys watching the Marlins game."

"Maybe Jessa ratted herself out," she replies with a snicker, but it's like the final piece of the puzzle falling into place.

That's it.

Holy shit.

"Fuck," I mutter, the pieces starting to fall into place. "Jessa messaged Tate."

Leni pauses and pulls back, meeting my intense expression. "Why would she do that?"

Why wouldn't she? She was going on and on during the ride to her place about how great we are together, even after I told her I wasn't interested. She was doing everything she could to keep me there, including grabbing my junk, a tactic that would have probably worked wonders at one time.

Before Leni.

"I had my phone when I was dropping her off. I remember because it was the first time I saw your text message," I recall, my mind spinning.

"Your phone?"

"Yeah, I lost it at some point. I think that was when I had it last. This morning, I couldn't find it," I state, telling her about running myself into exhaustion—twice—and my mom's visit at eight. "Son of a bitch. Jessa has my phone. She has to. That was when she had her hands all over me."

Leni's eyes narrow in annoyance. "I don't like her."

A bubble of laughter spills from my mouth. "Well, I do believe the feeling is probably mutual. Every time I mentioned you, she got that much more pissed off."

Leni cross her arms over her chest. "You know she fired me, right?"

I sit up straight. "What? When?"

"Monday morning. I barely made it out of my car when I got to her house. She met me in the driveway and told me she feared it would be too awkward when you dumped me and went back to her."

I lean forward once more and take her in my arms, pulling her onto my lap. "Not happening," I insist, resting my chin on her shoulder. "I didn't know she fired you."

She shrugs. "I didn't advertise it, partly because it does happen in my line of work, but also because I was trying to prove her words didn't affect me."

"But they did," I deduce, kissing the bare skin at the side of her neck.

"Yeah, a little."

I turn her to face me and almost groan when she leans back and swings her leg up and over my head so she's straddling me. Leni wraps her arms around my neck, pressing her chest into mine. "It's you and me against the world, okay? Nothing comes between us if we don't want it to."

She rocks forward, rubbing against my rapidly growing cock, the faintest grin playing at the corners of her mouth. "Deal."

"I'm serious, Leni. I'm not letting you go. How can I when I feel this way about you?"

"How do you feel?" she whispers, her breath fanning against my lips.

"I'm in love with you," I answer, watching as my words register on her gorgeous face. "I knew you were going to change my life the moment I stepped out of the shower and found you gawking at the goods."

Her eyes widen as she giggles and shakes her head. "You just had to go and ruin the moment."

"Oh, no. I saw it in your eyes. You don't have to lie to me. I know you appreciate my *assets*," I tease, flexing my hips upward into the apex of her legs.

Leni sighs and rests her cheek against me once more. "Malcolm?"

"Hmm?"

"Will you kiss me now?"

"It would be my absolute pleasure."

She meets me halfway, our lips finally touching after what feels like forever, when in reality it's been days. Leni opens her mouth, allowing my tongue to delve inside, savoring the feel of her against my lips and the taste of her on my tongue.

"Malcolm," she whispers, as I slide my lips across her cheek.

"Yes?"

"I love you too."

Something heady washes over me, bathing me in the most glorious feeling in the world. Happiness. Pure bliss. "Say it again."

"So bossy," she mumbles turning her head so I have better access to her neck.

"You like it when I'm bossy," I state, lazily dragging my tongue down the long column.

She sighs and rests her head on my shoulder. "I do."

"Come with me, Lenora. I want to sit and hold you on the couch for a bit."

She snorts. "Is that what the kids are calling it these days?"

A huge smile spreads across my face. "Why, Miss Abbott, I do believe your mind is in the gutter," I tease, standing up, her legs wrapping around my waist.

"Has been ever since I was cleaning City Hall and found the mayor standing in the bathroom without any clothes on."

I settle us down on the couch, her tucked comfortably and securely beneath me. "Best meet-cute ever."

She gives me that smile, the one that steals my breath and renders me speechless at the exact same time. "You know it."

EPILOGUE

Leni

Next Summer.

"Are you ready?" I ask Trace, who's chomping at the bit to get outside and help Malcolm. He's been in the backyard for the last thirty minutes, preparing for their father/son camping and fishing adventure.

It's the first annual event, sponsored by the Chamber of Commerce and Everything But Beer, where teams of fathers and sons get to camp and fish along the lake. There are prizes set in several different categories and is taking place over Father's Day weekend. Ever since Trace heard about it, he's been talking about this weekend.

Of course, now he has a little more flexibility to do the things he loves, since the water runs through our backyard. Trace and I moved in with Malcolm at the beginning of the year. It was the easiest adjustment, considering Trace and Malcolm were together almost every waking moment prior to him officially giving my son a bedroom in his home. And to be honest, it worked out great. We made a few scheduling adjustments to my work and the evenings I clean, Malcolm is home with Trace.

The only night we weren't able to adjust is Mondays, but that's okay. My mom and Alexandra, Malcolm's mom, take turns coming to the house to hang with Trace while I clean City Hall and Malcolm has his meetings. He hangs around until I'm finished, and then we go home together.

We've been very fortunate not to have to deal with Jessa much. Once Malcolm went to her house to retrieve his phone, he found all sorts of information on it. She used it to email Tate with the *MC Scoop*. She also had drafted a break-up text message to me but hadn't sent it yet. Why she didn't cover her tracks better is beyond me, but whatever. Malcolm used his position as a lawyer to politely convince her to get a retraction printed to try to repair the damage. Since, she's been hanging out in a neighboring town, rumored to be dating a man preparing to run for Congress.

Greg is still very much involved in his son's life too. He was actually here last weekend, along with his fiancée, Angelica, and her daughter, Molly. They come every month and stay at the apartment above the laundromat. We've gotten to know them over the course of the last year, having dinner together occasionally at the local restaurants, and inviting them to our home to celebrate major events like birthdays.

It's not always easy, but we make it work.

For Trace.

"I'm ready!" Trace hollers as he flies down the stairs and heads for the door.

"Wait right there, mister. Did you finish picking up all those Matchbox cars?" He nods. "Did you make sure your dirty clothes are put in the hamper and not strewn all over the floor?" He nods again. "You made your bed?" Nod. "And you're ready to have fun fishing and camping with Malcolm?"

"Yes!" he proclaims, so anxious to get out the door he's practically vibrating where he stands.

"Give me a hug and then go. Malcolm's ready to pitch the tent."

Trace throws his arms around me and mumbles, "Love you."

"I love you too," I reply, running my hand through his hair. "Go ahead."

He bolts out the door, leaving me standing in the kitchen, watching. I'm under explicit instructions not to come outside for anything. It's a boys' weekend, and since I'm a girl, I'm not allowed. Little does he know, after dinner, I plan on grabbing the new book my sister recommended, a glass of wine, and am hitting the hot tub for a little relaxation.

I stand there, one hip propped against the doorframe, and watch my two favorite people work together. They erect the tent, and Malcolm shows Trace how to build a fire in the pit. Once they have what they need set, they move to the dock to cast their first line. My heart is overflowing as they laugh. Malcolm is so patient and kind to my son, I have a hard time remembering he's real.

And he's ours.

I never expected to meet a man like Malcolm Wright, let alone fall in love with him. Now, I can't imagine my life without him. The way he loves my son, as if he were his own, yet shares him so easily with my ex, says a lot about the man he is.

The one I love.

Malcolm

The moment Trace falls asleep, I sneak out of the tent and go in search of Lenora. I heard her slip out of the house a bit ago and fire up the jets in the hot tub. All I can picture is her there, probably with wine and a book, and water cascading off her gorgeous curves.

I make sure the zipper is closed so no bugs get in and head for the place I know I'll find the woman I love. As I round the corner of the pergola, I find pay dirt. There she is. The most beautiful woman in the world, and she's all mine. I toe off my shoes and unbutton my shorts. I slip my T-shirt over my head before rounding the corner and coming into view.

"Enjoying a relaxing evening?" I ask stepping over the side of the tub.

Leni grins, her eyes zeroing in on my crotch, or specifically, to where my boxer briefs stretch tautly over my erection. "You're breaking the rules, you know. No girls during boys' weekend."

I head straight for her, taking the seat beside her and pulling her into my arms. "I missed you," I tell her, nuzzling my nose against her neck before I place a kiss on that delicate skin.

"I missed you too." She sets her book down on the side of the tub and throws her arms around my neck. "Having fun?"

"The best. I love spending time with him," I say, catching a whiff of the lotion on her skin.

"He loves hanging out with you too. It's the highlight of his day."

I reach over and take a small drink of her wine, needing something to do with my hand. "No, the highlight of his day is being with you. You're his mama, and he loves you more than anyone."

"Except when I make him clean his room," she replies, taking the glass and sipping the sweet white liquid inside.

"Even then. You'll always be his number one," I state, reaching for her left hand and running my thumb over the empty ring finger. My heart thunders in my chest as I prepare to do the one thing I've thought about doing since she moved in. Hell, since I met her. I knew we'd get to this place in life, one where we vow to love and cherish each other until death do us part.

The ring I bought her is on my own pinky finger, the delicate pear-shaped diamond turned to face my palm so she doesn't see it right away. I place my hand on her arm, making sure the diamond gently grazes her skin, and slide my hand up. She must feel the scrape and glances down in confusion. Slowly, I flip over my hand and show her what was rubbing against her arm. Her gasp fills my heart with excitement as I slip the ring off my own finger and hold it up between us.

"Leni, I didn't realize how shallow and unfulfilling my life truly was until I met you and Trace. Now, I don't want to imagine a day, a moment without you both in it. You make me a better man just by being you. I want to spend the rest of my life with you, help you raise your son, and maybe give him a few brothers and sisters."

I shift myself and reach for her hand, ready to slip the ring on it the moment she agrees. "Lenora Abbott, will you marry me?"

She smiles from ear to ear and nods. "Yes. I'd love to marry you."

I let out a whoop, slide the ring onto her finger, and pull her onto my lap. My mouth finds hers eagerly in a kiss that sets my blood on fire. "I love you, Lenora Abbott Wright."

She grins and bites down on her plump bottom lip. "Who says I'm taking your name? Maybe I want you to take mine?"

My hands slide to her ass and squeeze, my hips rocking upward, seeking the friction her body creates. "Whatever you want, baby. I'd gladly take your last name as long as it means we're married."

Leni rests her head on my shoulder and sighs. "I'll take your last name. There's no other name I'd rather have than yours."

"Soon. I want you to have it soon."

"Here. Let's get married in the backyard."

"Deal." I hold her close and just breathe her in. "Trace is gonna be pissed."

She sits up and meets my gaze. "Why?"

"He helped me pick out the ring, and then I didn't even let him help me give it to you."

Leni grins softly and returns her cheek to my shoulder. "I suppose we could do it again tomorrow so he's a part of it."

"Naw, that's okay. Now that the ring is on your finger, I don't even want to see you take it off. I'll just tell him I was so excited to spend the rest of my life with you and him, I couldn't wait to put it on your finger. He'll understand."

We sit there for several minutes with me toying with the sparkler she now adorns. "Do you know what sucks?" she asks, catching me off guard.

"What?"

"The fact we just got engaged, and we can't even go upstairs and celebrate because it's boys' weekend and I'm a girl."

I run my hand over her curves. "My favorite girl," I correct, kissing the back of her neck. "You know, I do have room in my sleeping bag for two."

"Really? But won't you get in trouble in the morning?"

"Oh, definitely," I reply with a laugh, "but it'll be worth his wrath."

And it was.

When Trace woke up the next morning and found his mom sleeping in the tent beside me, I took him outside so we could make her breakfast over the fire. Then, I told him I asked her to marry me, and she said yes. Trace cried, throwing his arm around my neck and telling me he loved me.

It was the start of something new.

The rest of our lives.

Who'd have thought it began with her bursting into my office bathroom. Well, that and the night at Pony Up. The one with the perfect kiss.

She changed my life, that's for sure.

And I can't wait to see what's in store for us for the rest of it.

The End

Enjoy the entire Mason Creek series!

Each book is a standalone featuring different Mason Creek residents.

Perfect Risk, book 1 – C.A. Harms
Perfect Song, book 2 – Lauren Runow
Perfect Love, book 3 – A.M. Hargrove
Perfect Night, book 4 – Terri E. Laine
Perfect Tragedy, book 5 – Jennifer Miller
Perfect Escape, book 6 – Cary Hart
Perfect Summer, book 7 – Bethany Lopez
Perfect Embrace, book 8 – Kaylee Ryan
Perfect Kiss, book 9 – Lacey Black
Perfect Mess, book 10 – Fabiola Francisco
Perfect Excuse, book 11 – A.D. Justice
Perfect Secret, book 12 – Molly McLain

Don't miss a single reveal, release, or sale! Sign up for my newsletter.
http://www.laceyblackbooks.com/newsletter

More Books by
LACEY BLACK

Rivers Edge series

Trust Me, Rivers Edge book 1 (Maddox and Avery) – FREE at all retailers

Fight Me, Rivers Edge book 2 (Jake and Erin)

Expect Me, Rivers Edge book 3 (Travis and Josselyn)

Promise Me: A Novella, Rivers Edge book 3.5 (Jase and Holly)

Protect Me, Rivers Edge book 4 (Nate and Lia)

Boss Me, Rivers Edge book 5 (Will and Carmen)

Trust Us: A Rivers Edge Christmas Novella (Maddox and Avery)

> ~ *This novella was originally part of the Christmas Miracles Anthology*

BOX SET – contains all 5 novels, 2 novellas, and a BONUS short story

With Me, A Rivers Edge Christmas Novella (Brooklyn and Becker)

Bound Together series

Submerged, Bound Together book 1 (Blake and Carly)

Profited, Bound Together book 2 (Reid and Dani)

Entwined, Bound Together book 3 (Luke and Sidney)

Summer Sisters series

My Kinda Kisses, Summer Sisters book 1 (Jaime and Ryan)

My Kinda Night, Summer Sisters book 2 (Payton and Dean)

My Kinda Song, Summer Sisters book 3 (Abby and Levi)

My Kinda Mess, Summer Sisters book 4 (Lexi and Linkin)

My Kinda Player, Summer Sisters book 5 (AJ and Sawyer)

My Kinda Player, Summer Sisters book 6 (Meghan and Nick)

My Kinda Wedding, A Summer Sisters Novella book 7 (Meghan and Nick)

Rockland Falls series

Love and Pancakes, Rockland Falls book 1

Love and Lingerie, Rockland Falls book 2
Love and Landscape, Rockland Falls book 3
Love and Neckties, Rockland Falls book 4

Standalone
Music Notes, a sexy contemporary romance standalone
A Place To Call Home, a Memorial Day novella
Exes and Ho Ho Ho's, a sexy contemporary romance standalone novella
Pants on Fire, a sexy contemporary romance standalone
Double Dog Dare You, a new standalone
Grip, A Driven World Novel
Bachelor Swap, A Bachelor Tower Series Novel
Perfect Kiss, Mason Creek Series #9

Burgers and Brew Crüe Series
Kickstart My Heart, book 1
Don't Go Away Mad, book 2

Co-Written with *NYT Bestselling* Author, Kaylee Ryan
It's Not Over, Fair Lakes book 1
Just Getting Started, Fair Lakes book 2

Can't Get Enough, Fair Lakes book 3
Fair Lakes Box Set
Boy Trouble, The All American Boy Series
Home To You, a second chance novella

Acknowledgments

What an absolutely amazing project to work on! First off, THANK YOU to my friend CA Harms for inviting to write in the Mason Creek world. It was so fun, and I've met some incredible authors along the way.

Thank you to all the authors in this joined world for making it a fun experience! Plotting residents, businesses, and character interaction was a huge part of what made this project so neat. I truly enjoyed working with each and every one of you and hope our paths cross again very soon!

My editing team – Kara Hildebrand, Sandra Shipman, Joanne Thompson, and Karen Hrdlicka. Thank you!!

The book team - Cover Designer, Opium House – Sarah Paige; Graphics Designer, Gel with Tempting Illustrations; Formatting, Brenda with Formatting Done Wright; and Promotions by Give Me Books and HEA PR. You are all the best of the best!

Kaylee Ryan, Holly Collins, Lacey's Ladies, and my ARC team, you are always right by my side, and I appreciate your help and guidance SO much!

To my husband and kids, thank you for not getting too mad when I lock myself in a room to write. It's not always easy, but we make it work!

To all the bloggers and readers, thank you, thank you, thank you. I hope you enjoy this story as much as I loved writing it.

AUTHOR

USA Today Bestselling Author Lacey Black is a Midwestern girl with a passion for reading, writing, and shopping. She carries her e-reader with her everywhere she goes so she never misses an opportunity to read a few pages. Always looking for a happily ever after, Lacey is passionate about contemporary romance novels and enjoys it further when you mix in a little suspense. She resides in a small town in Illinois with her husband, two children, and three rowdy chickens.

Website: www.laceyblackbooks.com
Email: laceyblackwrites@gmail.com
Facebook:
https://www.facebook.com/authorlaceyblack
Twitter: https://twitter.com/AuthLaceyBlack
Instagram:
https://www.instagram.com/laceyblackwrites/

Sign up for my newsletter so you don't miss a single sale, reveal, or release!
http://www.laceyblackbooks.com/newsletter